I0745277

The Inheritance

By Rafael Reyes-Ruiz

The Inheritance, by Rafael Reyes-Ruiz

Copyright © 2021 Jade Publishing, Machete Books

Cover: Photo by K Z on Unsplash.

First published in 2021 by
Jade Publishing
UNITED STATES OF AMERICA
P.O. Box 93341
Corpus Christi, TX.

www.jadepublishing.org

ISBN-13: 978-1-949299-19-9

Printed in the United States of America

Index

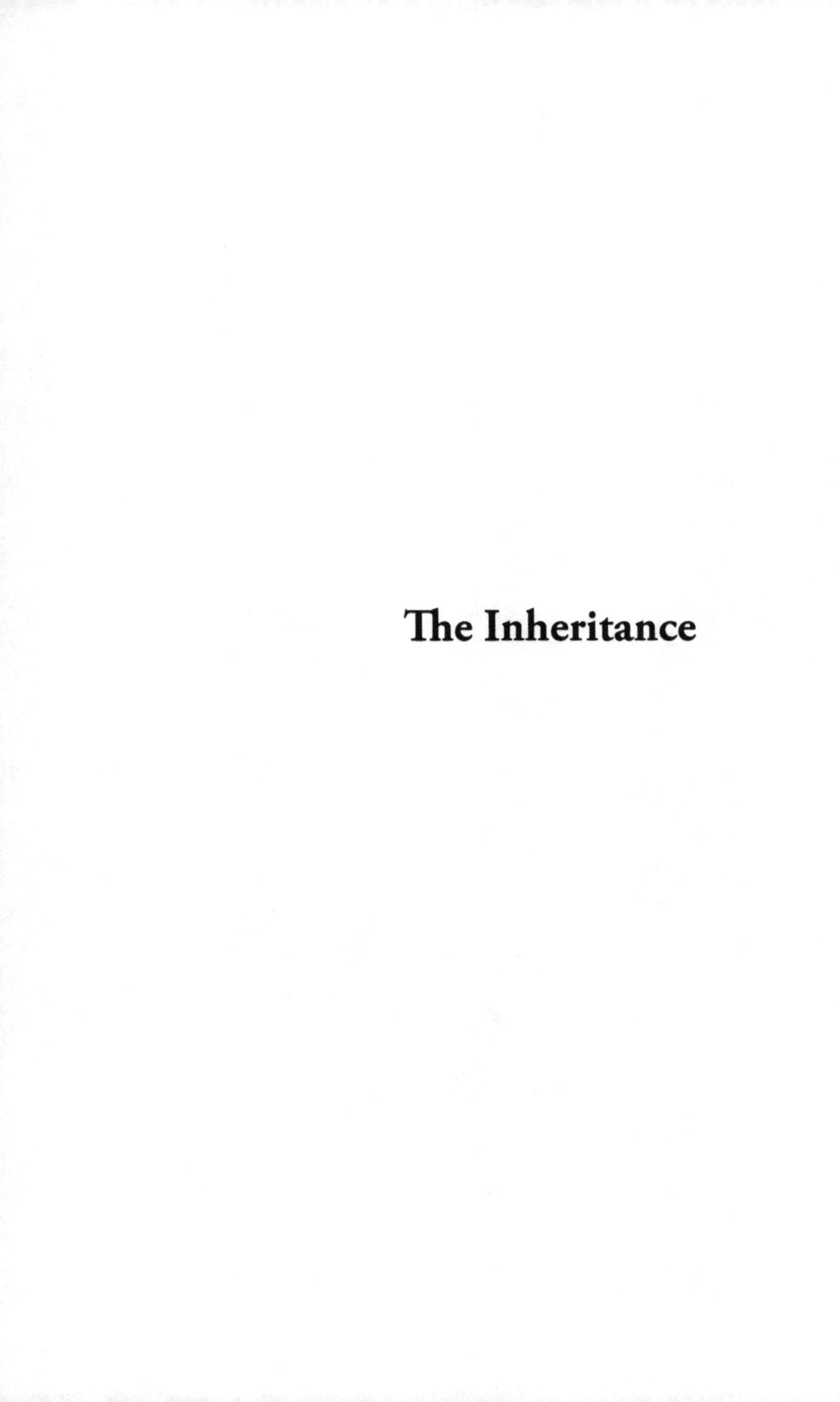

The Inheritance

ONE

It was not the first time Antonio, Tony, deplaned in Dubai; he had been there several times on his way to Japan and the United States. Today, though, Dubai was his destination, but he wasn't traveling there. Someone else was, or better said, it was he, but he had to act as someone else. Though he had slept during the flight from Tokyo, rather than being refreshed, he felt drowsy and not altogether there. He had the distinct feeling that only a part of him was driving his body, like he was sleepwalking.

At immigration, the officer scrutinized his passport and looked at him doubtfully. Prepared for this, Tony pretended to be embarrassed and told the officer that a medical treatment he'd recently undergone had left him bald. The truth was that he had shaved his head to avoid being recognized. The officer smiled and stamped his passport. All his documents were in order. Vladimir, one of his business partners in Japan, had taken care of the arrangements.

Tony had come to Dubai to be the manager of Sonatine,

a café restaurant in Bur Dubai, a neighborhood in the older part of the city. Vladimir had not given him many details; he had only said that if anyone asked, he was to say that he was implementing a new business plan and that if they wanted to know of his past experience say that he'd managed several restaurants in Tokyo, something that was not entirely untrue.

Tony did not like the idea of coming to Dubai, a place where he didn't know a soul and would feel lost. But Vladimir promised him he could hide quietly there—in plain sight—while the storm passed at work. He'd added, though, that he would have to be careful, and that he would have to keep a low profile and stay out of bars and nightclubs. Vladimir had been emphatic about it, pointing a finger at his face as a final warning. He reminded him that the *yakuza* had contacts everywhere. Tony knew that, if by any chance, Japanese Mafiosi visiting Dubai were to recognize him—a highly unlikely scenario—he could do nothing but immediately take off for Thailand or Colombia and hide in the home of one of his friends or relatives.

The apartment that Vladimir found him was on the fifth floor of the Chelsea Apartments. It had one bedroom and two bathrooms and was furnished in a style that could be called generic Ikea for the single man. In the living area, there was a sofa for two, a black leather recliner chair, and a dining table for four. In the bedroom, a king-size bed with a large framed photograph of the Eiffel Tower above it sat in the middle of the room. The rugs on the white-tiled floor had Mediterranean suns and beach motifs, which gave the apartment a holiday feel. From the living room panoramic window, he saw that the buildings on that street— and around the neighborhood for as far as he could see— were alternate versions of the Chelsea Apartments; mostly eight-storied with tinted windows and spacious balconies. On the ground floor of the building across the street, he saw the Sonatine, which had a neon sign with blue lettering and a treble clef as its logo.

The next day, as Vladimir had instructed him, Tony went to Sonatine for breakfast. It was a pleasant place, with ten to twelve tables and decorated in pastel colors with a musical theme, which reminded him of a trendy coffee shop in Tokyo. When Tony introduced himself to the two Filipino women behind the counter, the one in charge of the cash register, Vicky, told him that Mr. Vladimir had informed them of his arrival. She explained with a smile that expressed full complicity that she and her colleague took care of everything including the weekly accounting reports, which she would prepare for him. Vicky gave him a quick tour of the kitchen, and then took him to his new office, a well-appointed room with a view to the street. Vladimir had told him not to ask many questions and to simply say that all was in order, and that was exactly what he said.

When he returned to his apartment, Tony did one hour of yoga, as was his daily habit. When he finished, he threw himself on the couch and pondered how he would spend his time. In Tokyo, he would work eleven or twelve hours a day at the club in Roppongi, handling all kinds of unforeseen situations with customers and employees. The prospect of having no real responsibilities in Dubai was not at all attractive. He could not understand why he had to hide for so long. The problem was not with him but with Adriana, his former girlfriend and now business partner, who had allowed one of the new hostesses in their club to run away. Adriana had promised to pay the corresponding fine, though instead, she herself had also vanished. Now *he* was responsible for the whole mess in the eyes of the *yakuza* who controlled the clubs.

He did not want to think about that now. Adriana would show up eventually; perhaps she was getting the money for the fine. She'd told him, confidentially, that she would soon receive an inheritance from her grandfather, and he promised never to tell anyone. The inheritance had come to her suddenly, without her waiting for it. In any case, the inheritance should be at least fifty thousand dollars, equivalent to what was owed, if not more.

If indeed he didn't have to work, then he could read and do some translations. Tony was a fan of Soji Shimada, the former truck driver and famous author of detective novels. He had brought with him three of his novels and had bought five more from an online bookstore, which would arrive in a couple of weeks. His wish was that one day soon, in three years at the most and when he had enough money to not worry about anything, he could devote his time to translating Shimada's most successful novels into Spanish, which he was sure would sell like hotcakes.

Although he did not have to, Tony started going to Sonatine every day for two or three hours in the morning and at night, not to work but to read his books. After a few weeks, he realized that Sonatine had a tiny though loyal clientele. During the day, the clientele was mostly Levantine Arabs and some Emiratis who spent long hours drinking tea or coffee and talking on their mobile phones; Tony imagined that they were self-employed businessmen. At night, the clientele was mostly European and North American residents of the neighborhood who probably worked in office jobs during regular hours.

One of the most consistent customers was a somewhat disheveled tall redhead, who invariably ordered a salad niçoise or the soup of the day with bread, and a cup of black tea for dessert. From the first time he set eyes on her, Tony felt that she was a woman he could seduce. He thought—based on a furtive glance she cast when he passed by her table—that she found him attractive.

One night, he asked Vicky to let him work the cashier for a couple of hours and found out that the redhead was named Wendy Harold and that she had a gold credit card, which meant her monthly salary fell somewhere between four and six thousand dollars. This he knew because he had the same credit card and had read the footnotes of the credit application in which the salary requirements were listed. Things were easy for a skilled thief in Dubai, he considered; economic stratum was evident by the color of one's credit cards.

Later at home, he searched for Wendy on the net and found her on the website of the Dubai International University, an institution with faculty and administration from the Anglo-Saxon world. Her biography stated that she oversaw the International Exchange Program, something he found intriguing because the university did not admit foreign students. He looked at her CV and found that she had graduated from New York University in 1999 with a master's degree in comparative literature. That was eight years after completing her bachelor's in international studies from Macquarie University in Sydney, confirming his suspicion that she was, like him, around thirty-five years old. On closer inspection, he saw that she had written a thesis on urban imaginaries in the twentieth-century Japanese novel. The coincidence made him laugh.

***

One evening, while reading the newspaper on the couch at home, he saw Wendy return from the supermarket on the opposite street corner with two bags full of groceries. Before she crossed the street, Wendy stopped to chat with a European-looking man who had a long bushy beard that reached his chest. The man had a white terrier dog on a leash that was wagging its tail, apparently attentive to what they were saying. Tony remembered that he had seen the man at the Sonatine and that he seemed a fixture of the neighborhood.

He watched Wendy and the bearded man through his binoculars and tried to guess what they were talking about. Wendy had placed her shopping bags on the ground and was smiling at the man who gestured and pointed with his right hand towards the west, towards the new city of glass and steel skyscrapers. Tony surveyed the city and figured that they were talking about the construction projects that the local authorities had announced in the newspaper recently; a Taj Mahal replica that was four times larger than the original that was to be fitted with a shopping center, a hotel and a new urban development, which would house the largest shopping mall in the world.

Gazing toward the sea, Tony could make the outline of the residential towers on the palm-shaped artificial island that he had seen while riding one of those double-decker tour buses. It occurred to him that Adriana could be hiding in one of those condominiums. *Damned Adriana*, he thought. *Because of you I have to hide*. He returned the binoculars to the street corner and adjusted the lenses to better see Wendy and the bearded man who were still talking.

That night at the café, Wendy sat at a table facing his, and Tony thought she was glancing up at him. It was not the first time she stole looks, though this time he was sure that she was smiling on the sly, as if she knew he had been watching her. On impulse, he approached her.

"I'm Tony, the new manager. Welcome."

"Nice to meet you," Wendy replied, giving him a half smile that seemed to him full of irony.

"Are you Australian? I thought I detected a Sydney accent."

"Please, sit down. You have a good ear. Born and raised in Sydney, but my family is from the United States, from New York. And you?"

"Also from the U.S., though born in South America."

"Really?" Wendy's voice came loaded with a haughtiness that he found delicious.

They ordered a pot of chamomile tea with two cups and talked about life in New York. Tony said he lived in the city for nearly five years. Wendy seemed surprised and asked where he had lived and what he did for a living. He told her he lived in Astoria and worked in Manhattan as a translator.

"How interesting," Wendy noted. "English to Spanish?"

"No, Japanese to English."

"No kidding. I also speak Japanese. *Hajimemashite*."

"Oh, really? *Yoroshiku Oneigaishimasu*. How come?"

"Well, I went to school in Tokyo."

"You don't say. I also lived there as a student."

They talked about their favorite hangouts in Tokyo and other banalities. Tony noticed that Wendy was smiling a lot. It was then and there he knew that he would seduce her. He found himself fantasizing about kissing her. He could not help it as Wendy had a way of speaking. She leaned her head slightly forward—perhaps the habit of a woman who is taller than her average interlocutors, which he found charming and coquettish. Moreover, she enunciated her words so that she pouted every now and then, which made her lips extend as though they were an offering. Wendy must have felt the effect she was having on him as she started to look at him intently, following his eyes, which were often fixed on her lips. Suddenly, they began to talk about movies and discovered they both liked thrillers and that they both had seen Chinatown several times.

"I always watch it on the thirty-first of December," Wendy said.

"On that special night?"

"Somehow I always find myself alone on New Year's Eve," she said and then her face flushed.

Tony felt like he was falling into a trap, though it was a trap he was willing to fall into.

"Perhaps this year will be different," he said.

"How's that?" Wendy looked at him in the eye and smiled.

Tony paused, aware that what he was about to say would betray that he had fallen into the trap. New Year's was in two weeks, and in a flash, he saw himself with Wendy in his apartment, sharing a bottle of champagne.

"This year you may watch it in good company," he said, slightly leaning forward and lowering his voice.

Wendy gave him a wide smile. "I have work tomorrow, but it was nice to meet you," she said.

TWO

At about midnight after his evening walk beside the nearby cornice along the creek, which had been crowded with Indian and Pakistani families strolling and enjoying the cool evening air, Tony poured himself a double brandy to help him sleep. He looked at Sonatine from his window and remembered Wendy's expression before saying goodbye. A warm smile appeared on his lips and a pleasant tingle entered his stomach. He wanted to relive the playful banter with her, but when he tried to find the image of Wendy's smile what came to his mind instead was Adriana's face. He felt flustered and sat in full lotus on the sofa, preparing to meditate. But despite himself, Adriana's face came to his mind again, this time gesticulating at him in anger. He sipped on another brandy until he felt drowsy and went to bed. Later, he had a dream in which he felt he was awake.

He found himself in a narrow corridor that he needed to traverse to get to a place where a woman was waiting for him. His feet carried him forward, stepping one after another until he was in a full-blown run. He knew that at any moment he would wake up and not accomplish what he wanted, which was to possess the woman. He saw himself running towards a window he sensed was only a few steps away, and when he reached it, he plunged through the square space and into the void.

After a few seconds where all he heard was a deafening noise, he began to fly; a beautiful sensation that he had never felt before. He was in a city of identical buildings that looked like rectangular boxes with tiny square windows on a grid. It was surrounded by so many clouds that he could not see the ground. He saw an open window with curtains hovering in the air and felt certain that the woman was there. He entered through the window, his feet back on the ground, and found himself in another corridor. Oddly, it was the same corridor where the dream had begun, so he ran to look for the woman he sensed was waiting for him, but whom little by little, he realized, in spite of himself, was very far away from there.

He awoke suddenly and thought that he had slept for a long time, but the digital clock on the nightstand indicated it was half past midnight. He got up and went to the living room as if by reflex. Filtered through the curtains came the streetlights and the flickering *Diwali* decorations from the building across the street. He looked toward the supermarket and saw Wendy—dressed in a black evening dress and high heels—get into her car that was parked on the street. What was she doing out at this hour? Why was she dressed like that? Wendy put the car in reverse just as a black SUV with tinted windows smashed into her from behind, causing Wendy to crash into one of the parked cars in front of her. The crash made a loud, dry noise, and an instant later, the alarm of the other car went off. He saw clearly—and in slow motion—when the airbag from the steering wheel inflated and Wendy removed it from her face in a panic. He wanted to open the sliding door to the balcony to make sure that she was fine, but realized if he did, he would lose time; he had to get dressed and go downstairs right away to get help. He would tell the doorman to call an ambulance. He did not know the phone number for emergencies, though even if he had, he could not make the call himself as he had to avoid talking to the police. At that moment, when he was about to go to his room to get dressed, he saw a slight man in a white shirt and black pants—perhaps Indian or Bangladeshi—come out of the shadows of the parking lot of his building and rush to Wendy's car. He motioned frantically to her not to leave her vehicle—something she was about to do—and he went to the driver's window of the SUV. Tony didn't move. The man in the white shirt urged the driver of the SUV to open the window. After a few moments, the driver did. The man in the white shirt said something to him while pointing what seemed to Tony to be instructions for him to get out. Meanwhile, Wendy slipped out the passenger's door. The man realized that she was about to make a call on her mobile phone and yelled something that made her stop. The SUV's driver closed his window, started the car and left.

Who was the man in the white shirt? Tony felt he had to keep a cool head. He dressed quickly and went downstairs to the reception desk. The night guard was not there. On the street, he only saw Wendy's car. There was no sign of her or the man in the white shirt. He looked everywhere. To his left, he thought he saw two figures walking and entering an unlit patch of the road; one of the figures, the taller of the two, was limping slightly. It was them. He decided to follow discreetly. He put his hands in his pockets and started walking slowly, his gazed fixed on the unlit patch of street. He heard a voice from behind, and when he turned, he caught sight of a man—also wearing a white shirt—who was talking on a mobile phone while getting into Wendy's car. Who was that? The man parked her car in the spot where it was before the crash.

Tony decided that what mattered was not to lose sight of Wendy. If the second man in a white shirt had alerted the first man that someone was following them, he was putting himself in a potentially dangerous situation. He imagined what he would say if it became a police matter; that he had insomnia and was walking to relax and that he had not heard or seen anything out of the ordinary.

The two figures emerged from the unlit patch and crossed the street. The slight man in the white shirt was talking on his mobile. Oddly, he felt he had done this before, that it was not the first time he had followed Wendy. Though, he had only done that with his binoculars whenever he caught sight of her on her routine trips to the supermarket and Sonatine. They walked down several streets he did not know and that looked identical to his own. On one of them, there was a Chelsea Apartments II, a Dorchester and other buildings with London names. Where the man in the white shirt was taking Wendy, he had no idea. He imagined that Wendy was in some sort of trouble. They crossed a broad avenue and he realized they were near the Bank Street intersection. Vladimir had told him not to go there at night because the area was under heavy surveillance. He felt a little afraid. What he was doing was absurd! What happened to Wendy was not his business. Wendy was not Adriana. Adriana was not Wendy. He saw Wendy and her companion enter the 24-hour supermarket on the avenue. He would go there and buy something. That would be his limit; then he would go home.

As he entered the supermarket, he saw Wendy talking to two European-looking men. They were dressed in evening clothes like Wendy's as if they had been or were going to a party. The man in the white shirt was gone. Tony bought a bottle of mineral water and paid cash. Wendy and the two men looked as though they were about to go out into the street though they did not move. They were waiting for someone or for a car to pick them up. Wendy was safe and that was all Tony cared about right then. He was certain—though it was an intuitive certainty—that the men who were with her were her friends. At that moment, another woman entered the store and started to chat with them animatedly. A blonde, Russian or Baltic, tall and gorgeous like a model. Tony looked at her carefully; she was wearing a blue satin evening dress and wore professionally applied makeup with lots of eyeliner, like an exotic dancer in Roppongi or an expensive escort. He felt a chill run from his lower back to the nape of his neck. This *is* business, he thought. For a moment he felt disoriented, as if he were back in Roppongi on the street of the high-end nightclubs. He did a double take as though his eyes had deceived him, but the blonde was still there, talking to Wendy and the two men. His instinct told him to disguise himself and quietly disappear. He covered his forehead with one hand and turned around when he realized that only Wendy would be able to recognize him, and her back was turned to him. A moment later, a black SUV with tinted windows, identical to the one that crashed into Wendy's car, arrived, and the group of four climbed into it and disappeared.

The days after the crash, Tony did nothing but think about what had happened that night. Wendy had not shown up at Sonatine since then, and he had not seen her anywhere. He kept repeating to himself that it was none of his business, though without wanting to, he was fixating on the events. He somehow associated the whole thing with Adriana, with Adriana's disappearance that had actually been an escape. His head was a mess. Vladimir had written to tell him to continue to remain in hiding and not to go out at night. *Be careful,* he wrote in capital letters. *Don't let yourself get into anything. Nothing. The staff at Sonatine can help you with whatever you need.* Still, Tony could not stop thinking about Wendy. He conjectured that she was hiding, though he was aware that this conjecture was based on a dubious premise, probably one that was false. Why would she do that? Wendy worked at a university, or did she? Did she do something else?

Tony thought that the bearded man whom he observed Wendy speaking to the other day could give him some information. He sensed that he was someone who noticed everything that happened in the neighborhood. He decided that when he spoke with him, he would be careful. The afternoon was spent at home reading and waiting for five o'clock when the bearded man would walk around the block with his dog. After exercising his companion, he stood at the corner, perhaps to rest or to enjoy the cityscape.

The sky was filled with wisps of high clouds like bold brush strokes of faded white paint that were slowly turning orange. When Tony approached him, the man smiled broadly and said good afternoon, as if he was expecting him. They began talking about the weather.

"The evenings are turning cold," the man said.

"Not as cold as in Europe!"

"Yes, you're right. I'm no longer used to it. I'm Dutch. Where are you from?"

"Miami," Tony replied.

"Miami? Dubai reminds you of home, right?"

"Well, yes and no. Miami has a Latin flavor, and Dubai an Indian one."

"Indian flavor? Interesting point. You live in the Chelsea, right?" The man bent down to pet his furry friend.

Tony nodded and looked at the dog that was panting and wagging its tail.

"Forgive me for being nosy," the man added. "I live in the Savoy and spend a lot of time with Charlie walking about."

They talked of the best places to walk around the neighborhood, and of the nearby creek and the cornice where the bearded man said he went for a stroll in the early morning to see the dhows and other small boats sailing in and out. The bearded man had a very friendly conversational manner and looked at Tony with curiosity, though in a kind way. At some point it got dark, and the light show on the Burj Khalifa tower, roughly a mile to the west, began. The bearded man asked him what he thought of the world's tallest building. He recalled that every time he saw the red and white lights rise from the ground floors to the tapered middle and then on to the needle at the top, he was reminded of a giant syringe injecting liquid light into the sky. But he did not say that to the bearded man; it was a metaphor that somehow revealed too much about him; his way of seeing the world.

"It reminds me of the Tower of Babel in a medieval book," he said.

"You mean in Kircher's manuscript? What a coincidence," said the bearded man. "I've been studying it recently. It's online, you know?"

Tony nodded, saying yes, and thought the bearded man would tell him all he needed to know in due time.

"But tell me" the old man said, an expression of surprise on his face, "why are you interested in medieval manuscripts?"

"Well, I'm just curious about them. I like fantastic maps."

"Is that so? Another coincidence. My name is Robert Deenik, and I'm a history professor at the Dubai International University. Can I offer you a drink? I have liquor for every taste."

***

Deenik's apartment was on a corner and had a panoramic view of the city. Several carpets of different designs, colors and sizes covered the entire tiled floor. The furnishings were Indian and made of fine woods with cotton and silk cushions. They sat on a couch watching the skyline that seemed drawn on the horizon with threads of white, yellow and red lights. They talked about the map in Kircher's manuscript, which brought them back to the Burj Khalifa Tower and to skyscrapers in general. At some point Deenik said that Dubai was a fantasy. Although a little later, he said it was a *simulacrum* and remained silent for a moment, perhaps seeking the thread of an argument that he wanted to put forth.

"Forgive me for being so cryptic," he said and let out a short laugh. "Don't take me too seriously—at the university we talk about Dubai all day."

Since Deenik had mentioned the university, Tony asked about Wendy.

"Wendy? She has an office in the library. Why do you ask?"

"I'm just curious. Wendy always has dinner at Sonatine, and we haven't seen her in a few days."

Deenik scratched his neck as if thinking about something. "Yes, now that you mention it, I have not seen her these last few days either. She may be attending a conference. She travels a lot. I did speak with her the other day, and she didn't mention anything, though that doesn't surprise me."

"Why is that? Tony tried to sound casual, but he realized he came off as concerned.

"Well, Dubai is like a revolving door; so many people come and go. Very few stay long enough for anyone to get to know them. It's not unusual in this country, you know."

Tony waited in silence for clarification, but Deenik added nothing more. He poured them another round of scotch.

"Wendy has an odd work title, the kind that makes you think it's a front, a façade," Deenik said with a grin. "But I'm speculating again. Do forgive me; it's the way I work. It gets me to the core of things. Wendy is very reserved. I've always had the impression that she keeps cards up her sleeve, a bit like you, if you'll excuse me for being so blunt."

***

The following day, Tony did not leave the apartment. He had breakfast and a light lunch delivered from Sonatine with the pretense that he was not feeling well. He was in good health, though had an odd feeling. His discomfort around not knowing Wendy's whereabouts compounded his anger over Adriana's disappearance. He thought about the last time he had seen Adriana, and what came to mind was Wendy's expression when she had said that she watched Chinatown every December thirty-first. It occurred to him that there was something hidden in that phrase, a clue that he had to decipher—though he could not think of what it could be.

He closed his eyes, wishing to conjure up Adriana's face but what came to his mind was the moment the *yakuza* gangster walked into his office at the club to tell him that Adriana and her friend had taken off. He had not believed it at first, but later that night, one of the new Colombian dancers told him she saw Adriana pack her bags and leave the building where most of the foreign hostesses and dancers lived. It occurred to him that Adriana had come to Dubai and that she now worked for Wendy. Though he realized an instant later this was an unlikely scenario because the *yakuza* kept Adriana's passport, and she could not get out of the country, at least not so soon.

Still, it would be interesting if the two women knew each other and worked together, and both desired him as much as he desired them. He threw himself on the sofa and let the fantasy take him. Instantly he felt guilty, which was something he had wanted to avoid. He reflected and realized that he felt this way because he had made a mistake. He had let Adriana become his partner, and she had failed to deliver. Yes, it was his fault. She had not been ready. The *yakuza* were looking for him to punish him for it.

They were looking for him in the wrong place. Only Vladimir and his friend, Pablo, a Peruvian of Japanese descent, knew of his whereabouts. He trusted the two of them completely. Tony was in Dubai, and Dubai was a fantasy or a *simulacrum* or whatever, although for him it was purgatory. Wendy was not Adriana. She was another woman that made him feel as Adriana had once made him feel; something beyond desire, something closer to longing, something that contained a promise.

The call to prayer from the neighborhood mosque took him out of his musings. Through the window, he saw a red dot, and when he squinted, he first saw the tip of a lit cigarette and then the man who smoked it. It was a man in a white shirt looking at the street, like the man the other night. A man, like himself, given the responsibility of keeping things in order, to make sure nothing bad or out of the ordinary happens. It was a difficult job because there was always the unexpected; cars that crashed, people who needed help because they had to flee or hide or because they possessed a secret, a clue, or a key to something. He had just arrived in this city. He was just beginning to get into the swing of things. It would take time to learn who was who, and most importantly, who was pulling the strings.

THREE

The Uber dropped them off at the entrance to the *Music Room*, a nightclub and concert hall next to a four-star hotel in Bur Dubai. It was the first time that Adriana Paola, who in Dubai preferred to be called just Paola, went to that part of the city. It was one of the oldest, as the Pakistani driver had said. She felt tense and insecure. It was always like this when she went to a place that she didn't know and was beyond her comfort zone. The neighborhood was not like where she lived with Esperanza; in a luxury apartment overlooking the sea and surrounded by equally luxurious apartment towers. It was near a shopping mall that had the best brand-name stores, and where there was also an indoor ski resort, and Italian and French restaurants. In this neighborhood the buildings were shorter and less elegant. The streets were also narrower, and most of the people walking around were darker; you could hardly see any Europeans or Americans. She imagined that some were Pakistanis, like the driver, or perhaps Indians or Bangladeshi, and others from several Asian countries, from the Philippines and China.

She needed a drink to warm up, but she thought it best not to go to the bar right away, and instead to wait a little and let Esperanza, her cousin—whom she loved as a sister and knew how things were in that city—take the initiative. Esperanza was, for the moment, her guardian angel, her fairy godmother, who guided her and cared for her in what, to her, was a new world. The fact that she was in Dubai was providential, a stroke of luck. Esperanza had called her in Tokyo to wish her a happy birthday and to invite her to spend a few days of vacation at her place. Just when she was in need of a spot where she could spend some time without anyone knowing of her whereabouts—six months at least—until she could make arrangements to cash in on her inheritance, pay off the debts she had, and decide what new direction to take.

The club was cavernous, a rectangular enclosure, like some sort of warehouse. It was painted black with beer neon lamps as decor and a stage for live performances in the back. The tall industrial-style circular tables reminded her of one of her favorite clubs in Tokyo, where she had spent so many nights with her party friends.

It was still early, about ten o'clock, and some of the tables near the stage were already taken.

"Are we all Colombian here?"

"No sweetie," her cousin replied and gave her a little pat on her back. "Like I told you, this is a *Latino* event," she added in a lower voice. "The organizers are Ecuadorian, but there are also Mexican, Argentines, Chileans, Venezuelan, and Colombians, of course."

"And we're safe here?"

"Yes, sweetie, don't worry; this city is very safe, nobody here is looking for you."

"You never know."

"Should we get a tequila?"

"Yes, cousin, I need one."

"The bar is the other way," Esperanza said. When she turned around, she had to grab a table to steady herself; she almost lost her balance maneuvering in the new stilettos that Paola had given her as a gift.

At the bar, there were two men talking when they arrived; one of about their age, around thirty. He was of Mediterranean looks with a tanned complexion and dark hair, wearing a suit and white shirt without a tie. The other was dark, in his fifties, with straight salt and pepper hair. He wore jeans and a white linen shirt. The young man stood up and turned around; he had seen them in the mirror. The other also turned but remained in his chair.

"Hi Esperanza," the younger man said. "You look gorgeous with your blonde hair! And in very good company with your twin."

"Hi Fernando," Esperanza replied and kissed him on the cheek. "I thought you were flying this weekend."

"The helicopter's electrical system broke down. I'm on holiday until they fix it. This is Esteban Garrido, a well-known lawyer and businessman who's been in Dubai for a few years."

"And this is Paola, my beloved cousin. She works with me at the agency. She helps me with the accounting. She's just arrived from Europe, from Madrid."

Esperanza told Esteban that it was a pleasure to meet him, and that she had heard about him through some Colombian musician friends who worked in a beachfront hotel. Esteban said yes, of course. They were very good friends of his. He had also heard about her and congratulated her for her success.

"Do you have models from several countries?" he asked.

"Mostly from Belarus, Ukraine, and Russia, but we also count with some Colombians and Brazilians," Esperanza replied, digging from her wallet a business card that she handed to Esteban. "We also have girls who work as hostesses for any kind of event, commercial or private. We work every day, including Fridays and holidays. We are at your service."

"I can vouch they provide first class service," Fernando said and nodded twice, his gaze fixed on Esteban, as if his endorsement or support were required at that moment.

Esteban took the card and looked at it front and back; the back was written in Arabic. "I'll stop by your office in a few days," he said. "I am organizing a small event and we could use some hostesses to help us with logistics."

"Of course," Esperanza replied. "It would be a pleasure to work with you, I mean, with both of you too," she said, looking at Fernando.

"How about shots of tequila to celebrate?" Esteban asked.

"It's just what we need," Paola replied, and she took Esperanza's hand, who smiled from ear to ear.

When the drinks were served, Fernando commented that it was important for Latinos to help each another in Dubai, a city where there was a lot of competition in business and in the professions.

"When I first came here ten years ago," he said, "most of the helicopter pilots in Dubai were European, and many of them knew each other; one recommended the other and so on. I was lucky because one of my instructors in Colombia knew the manager of the company where I work now, a Lebanese with very good connections to one of Dubai's most prominent sheikhs. Now that I know how things work, I've been able to bring three of my colleagues from Colombia."

Esperanza said that with her it had been something similar. That in her case it had been a friend of hers who was a model and had married an Emirati who owned an employment agency in Dubai, and that thanks to their help—and to God—she had come and set up the agency, which had done very well so far.

"Dubai is the perfect city for the sort of services we offer, she added. "That said," she looked at her mobile that had just vibrated and frowned. "I have to take this," she said, and got up, rushing towards the door.

After Esperanza walked out, Fernando said that he had met her at an event that one of the sheikhs of Dubai organized a few years ago. He told them about a romance that started between one of Esperanza's Russian models and a guest at the party that he claimed was a *typical* Dubai story. The guest was a middle-aged American executive who worked at the Dubai office of a multinational corporation. He apparently fell head over heels in love with the model and started dating her and buying her expensive gifts such as brand-name gold watches and platinum jewelry. The couple married after a few weeks. After three or four months, the young woman said she needed a substantial amount of money to pay for some medical treatment for her father who lived in Russia. The executive gave her the money, and the young woman flew to Moscow. A few days after, the young woman called her husband to tell him that she was never coming back to Dubai and that she had had a change of heart and wished him good luck in the future. Rumor had it that the executive was an abusive husband who constantly belittled the young woman for being a model, and that her leaving him was her revenge. Shockingly, it was also revealed that the executive was still married to his first wife back in the United States. Upon learning of her husband's double life in Dubai, she asked for a divorce, and the court ruling left him practically bankrupt.

While Fernando told the story, Paola threw glances at Esteban who seemed amused with its twists and turns. She felt attracted to him. His face was round and good-natured, his eyes gray and piercing. His hands were long and thick and well-groomed as if he recently had a manicure. That he was a lawyer surprised her; she would not have guessed. To her, he looked like a wealthy rancher, the owner of a large hacienda, someone used to the outdoors, and country living.

When he finished telling the story, Fernando looked at his watch and made a face of surprise. He then said he had to go talk to some of the event's organizers, so he begged to be excused and added that he would look for them later. Before leaving he approached Esteban and whispered something in his ear, which made him laugh. Although there was quite a lot of noise in the bar—by then, several couples had taken the bar stools around them and talked animatedly— Paola could hear Esteban saying that the deal would yield great profits, and that they should discuss later how to do it again. For some reason, Paola thought that it was something about jewels, probably Colombian emeralds. It was a hunch, a matter of instinct; she had experience with men like Esteban, and she was rarely wrong.

Esteban suggested that they sit at a table and chose one in a corner in the back where there were fewer people. The background music, which until now had been romantic salsa, faded to a stop. A DJ, a skinny guy wearing a fedora hat, took the stage where his gear had been set up, and in English with a heavy Indian accent, encouraged the audience to enjoy the latest Latin hits and take to the dance floor.

After ordering drinks, Esteban asked Paola why she left Madrid.

"The Madrid gig was temporary, a short-term contract,"

she replied. She fixed her bangs with her hands as she felt they were covering her forehead completely. "My work with Esperanza in Dubai is much better, more interesting," she added.

"Do you like Dubai?"

"It's a very interesting city," Paola said.

"In what sense?"

"It seems to me that it is not one city but several, do you know what I mean?"

"As if instead of going from one neighborhood to another it's like you're going from one country to another?"

"That's it," Paola replied. "I see that I'm not the only one who has that impression. How long have you been here?"

"It'll be five years in December, but they have passed quickly."

Paola looked Esteban in the eye and told him that he looked like someone who traveled a lot.

"Yes, quite a bit," he said. "Not so much in this region, but mostly in Asia."

Paola felt a knot in her stomach and asked, "Did you spend much time in Japan?"

"Never been there," he said and took a sip of his drink. "But someday I'll visit the *Empire of the Rising Sun*," he added with some emphasis. "I feel drawn to oriental culture, Buddhism, Ying and Yang, and so on."

"Where are you from?" Paola asked. There was something in Esteban that didn't add up. She sensed that he was lying to her, perhaps because he was hiding something or because he was playing with her.

"You don't think I'm Colombian, do you? I don't have an accent, right?"

"Your accent is from nowhere. That's why I'm asking you."

"I was born in Miami, but my parents are Colombian. I lived a few years in Bogotá, where I finished high school."

"And then you got into the military?"

"Excuse me?"

"You look like military or police."

"Military or police?" Esteban said in a low voice as if to himself and huffed out a laugh.

"And you look as someone who's never been to Madrid," he added and drummed his fingers on the table.

"I know Madrid like I know my hometown," she said, a grimace on her face. She put both hands on the table as if she was ready to get up and leave. "Don't change the subject," she added in a loud whisper. "Are you in the military or in the police? Yes or no."

"Yes and no," Esteban replied. "I've never been in the police force," he added. "I studied law at the Military Academy in Bogotá, and I was a military officer many years ago, but now I am retired, and I work for a private company."

"A military company?"

Esteban made a wry face, and said that he would tell her about his job if she told him why she left Madrid.

"You first," Paola replied.

"I like you, so I'll tell you," Esteban said and leaned towards her as if he were going to share a secret. "But only if you promise me—a real promise—that you won't go around telling everyone."

Paola nodded her head.

"Let's toast first," Esteban said and raised his glass.

"And may a thunderbolt strike you if you lie," she quipped.

"I am a private contractor for a security company."

"And I'm Cinderella," Paola said.

"The real Cinderella?" Esteban made a face of disbelief.

"Yes, really. I'll tell you later. But, wait. What precisely is a security company?"

"Let me explain," he said and again leaned towards her. "The company I work for is in charge of the security of some strategic locations in Dubai."

"A security guard company," Paola said and looked at the stage. A middle-aged man wearing a linen suit was holding a wireless microphone in his hand. He was in the middle of saying something, but there was no sound.

"Something like that, but at a higher level," Esteban explained, "I work in the legal department and have to liaise with colleagues in other countries; England, South Africa, and Colombia, in my case."

"I get it," Paola said. "Like the security company that protected diplomats in Iraq during the war that now has its headquarters in Dubai."

"You hit it on the nail. But that has to remain between the two of us. Don't tell anyone, okay?"

"I am a tomb," Paola said. She remembered that someone in Tokyo had told her that this security company recruited Colombian mercenaries to work in the Middle East, in the Emirates and Saudi Arabia, if she remembered correctly. If what Esteban said was true and he worked with the legal department of such a company, he would have to be as wily as a fox, something that, in her eyes, made him very attractive. She had always liked lawyers; the wilier the better.

The man on the stage, microphone in hand, thanked everyone for coming and named some companies that sponsored the event; a chain of French supermarkets and a couple of local travel agencies. Before leaving the stage, he said that he was sending special regards to Don Esteban Garrido, and with the microphone, made as if to toast and looked in their direction. One of the stage lights fell on them.

Esteban raised his glass and without speaking mouthed to your health, and that they would talk later.

"You are a celebrity here," Paola said.

"The guy's a good friend, but as you can see, he's not very discreet."

"So, you are not incognito. You don't have to protect your identity?"

"Not at all," Esteban replied. "Why do you ask me that?"

"Don't mind me. I'm just thinking out loud."

Esteban's mobile phone rang, and he said he had to take it. He got up and walked a few paces away. Paola looked around for Esperanza; she thought it strange that she'd left her alone for so long. The place was almost full of people, mostly young Latin American professionals that were in pairs or in mixed groups, similar to some of the Latin events in Tokyo. There were several tables of only women, though from their looks they were not women of her *scene*. Although they could very well be, Dubai was a different market with different rules.

"It's your turn to tell me your story," Esteban said when he returned to his seat.

"Let's say that I am a businesswoman who at the moment is working in accounting."

"And you managed models and hostesses in Madrid?"

"In Tokyo, actually."

"I think we're finally making progress," Esteban said and made the peace sign with his fingers, which Paola thought odd. It turned out to be an order for two more tequilas to a waitress who was coming to their corner.

FOUR

Paola woke up suddenly, breathing heavily; she was coming out of a nightmare in which she was drowning in a lake or river, in a cold and forgotten place. When she calmed down, she realized that she was not in Esperanza's apartment, but in a hotel room. Probably in the hotel next to the club, but she didn't remember how she got there. Her head hurt a little. Light came in through the half-closed curtains, but it was the reflection of a neon sign, not the light of day. What time was it? She was going to look next to her but felt afraid of what she would find. Why didn't she remember anything? She closed her eyes and a memory came to her of someone opening the door to a room and speaking. It was Esperanza asking her if she was ok. She looked at her side and realized that no one had slept with her; the blanket on the other side of her bed was intact, as well as the pillows. Esperanza was asleep in the other double bed with her mouth open and her hands folded under her head, as if in prayer. She looked like a little angel about to sing.

Her mobile was on the bedside table. It was five past one.

Apart from the headache, she also felt a little dizzy. *Who knows how many tequila shots I had*, she thought, *or when and how I lost control, if I had lost it.* She was a good drinker. In Tokyo, she was always the last person sober in any group, especially with the Japanese. But Esteban was an inveterate drinker, a long-shot drinker as they said in back home in Tocaima. She remembered they danced together to an oldie he liked, and that they returned to their table and ordered more tequila.

And after that? Yes, they had laughed at something, at a story that Esteban told her; something absurd that happened to him in France, or was it in Senegal? He traveled a lot. He said that he'd been in the French Legion, and at first, she thought he'd said the French *Religion*. She'd told him she didn't know what the French Legion was, and Esteban didn't believe her initially. He said, how was that possible, and that everybody knew about it. She had said that they had not been introduced, and the two burst out laughing. Paola had felt light and euphoric, as she had not felt in a long time. Later on the dance floor, when they played yet another song that he liked, she did a couple of Bollywood moves, which she'd learned from one of the models at the agency; a British girl of Indian descent, or was it the other way around? Esteban was not a good dancer, but he kept up and didn't take his eyes off her. At some point, she'd fantasized about going to a hotel with him and playing one of her favorite games; she would tie him up to the bed and bandage his eyes.

That had not happened. She would remember it. It was something she only dared to do when she was completely sober. What she remembered, now that she put her mind to it, was a conversation about why they lived where they lived, and why they did what they did for a living. He had married and divorced young and had a son who lived in Miami with his mother who was from Puerto Rico and was a registered nurse. She told him that it was a coincidence that she had also studied Nursing. She had lied to him because explaining that she'd only had a Nurse's Aide degree would make her look less than his ex-wife, and that night she didn't want any comparisons.

Esteban told her that after their divorce, which had not been very friendly, they hated each other. In fact, he'd joined the French Legion and spent several years in French Guiana, something that also made her laugh, not because she didn't know that there was a country called that—she had gone to school, and she knew the capitals of many countries—but because that night everything had 'French' in it. She knew a French woman in Tokyo who was a high-class hostess and worked in a private club in Roppongi. Every time she heard the word 'French' she thought of her, who—apart from being pretty—was perverse. She liked to mistreat men; she would slap them in the face if they looked at her for too long. A strange woman indeed, but in the end one of the few friends she had.

And after that? Ah yes, when it was her turn, she told him about her hometown, and about the *babillas* in the artificial lake on the main square that tourists confused with alligators. Also about the hot springs near her house and the fruit trees in the backyard. And about the boyfriend she had when she turned fifteen who had a Paso Fino horse worth millions, and how he joined a paramilitary unit that fought the leftist guerrillas in the north, which for some reason had made him very rich; he had cash coming out of his nostrils, townspeople would say. Talking about that had made her nostalgic, and she had downed another tequila.

Esteban told her not to worry, and that the night was for reminiscing. She'd felt comfortable and at ease as if

Esteban was a lifelong friend. Then, she told him about what had happened to her; the trap she'd fallen into, and an edited version of how she'd gotten out of it. How she'd gone to Japan thinking that she was going to work in a nursing home, but that it had turned out to be a hostess gig in a bar. She had to pay back all the money she owed, plus interest, for them bringing her to Japan, not to mention a bonus for what those cynical jerks called "representation expenses." That was what she told Esteban, and what she'd told Esperanza when she arrived in Dubai. It was a half-truth that she repeated so often that she had started to believe that the woman who had to work as a strip-tease dancer in that creepy theater in Kabukichō was someone else, and not her; somebody foolish and naïve.

Esteban told her that he knew what the hustle was like in Tokyo, some friends had told him, and asked her what she had done. She told him that she had paid off her debt and become independent. At the end of a year she had saved enough money to send to her parents to cover some of the debts they had, and still had money left over for her to come to Dubai to work with her cousin. She wanted to help her with what she could. After all, she was family, and family came first.

What happened afterward she couldn't really say. Very likely she had suddenly fallen asleep. She was like that when she drank a lot; she was not one of those drunks who makes a fuss and breaks glasses or dishes or starts to sing out of tune. What else had happened? Oh yes, Esperanza had found her in the bathroom of this very room, and she was crying. She cried because she thought of Tony, her partner, who had helped her out of the hole. Tony with whom she fought every day even though she loved him. Tony who was probably in Bangkok right now with his buddies or with some Thai girl. Tony was a womanizer; she always told him he was a dog, a bad dog, and he would laugh and would start barking at her. Woof, woof.

She looked again at her mobile. She wasn't sleepy anymore, but instead was wide awake. There was a new message in her email box. Perhaps it was what she was waiting for; news from home. She figured it would be from her Dad who would have read the email she had sent to a friend who lived in the same neighborhood. But the message was from her mother and from an email account bearing the name of a relative in Bogotá! She felt like shouting but covered her mouth as she didn't want to wake Esperanza, at least not now. It was the first time her mother wrote to her; they always talked on the phone, but those were uncomfortable calls in which she had to pretend that everything was fine. That she was doing great at work, and that she missed them very much, which was the only thing that was true.

My daughter, my baby, the message began. *How are you? I'm so happy to hear nothing bad happened to you. At home we do nothing but worry about you. We heard from one of your friends that you left Japan, and we were worried sick, but then, two days later, we heard from another friend in the neighborhood that you were in Dubai with Esperanza! We were so happy to hear that. Esperanza is a fine young woman, and she can help you with whatever you need. It's a pity that her mother and father were taken by the war and are no longer in this world.* Adriana paused for a moment. She closed her eyes and heard her mother's voice saying to her what she'd just read and felt tears come to her eyes.

We are running the errands, she went on. *Who would have imagined that Grandpa Rafael's stuff was so valuable? We had no idea that he'd written to you on his own. We thought that the old man's dementia was quite advanced, and he couldn't write by himself. Your dad and I believe it was a miracle from God. I'm in Bogotá, staying with Cousin Carmen who's helping me. She sends you a hug; she is very happy that you are safe and sound. You know she always asks about you, and she worries when I don't hear from you. Yesterday, we went to the museum and talked to the director as you suggested, although it was not the Ms. Medina that Grandpa Rafael mentioned. She passed away a few years ago, but it was a Dr. Cruz, a doctor in museology, and a very kind sweet woman. When I showed her the little bargueño, she looked at it in surprise. She brought a magnifying glass and a few small bottles of liquids and examined every nook and cranny. She put a few drops from one of the small bottles on the back of the drawers, and then on the wooden veneers. After all that, she told us that it was probably an authentic sixteenth or seventeenth century piece, but that they had to do other tests to be sure. She told us that she and the museum experts could go to Tocaima to see the other bargueños next week. I showed her the photos of the whole lot and asked her how much it could be worth. She said she didn't know, and that the experts would do the assessment so we would have to wait at least three weeks. However, she told us that the little one we showed her could be worth anywhere from ten to twenty thousand dollars. Go figure!*

But the story does not end there. That afternoon a woman called and said that she'd heard that we had some old bargueños, though she couldn't tell us who from, and that she was interested in buying them. She asked me if she could drop by the house to talk. I told her I need to talk it over, you know how things are in this country, so I told her to call back in an hour. Cousin Carmen searched the Internet and found out that she has her own web page where it says she's Colombian but naturalized in Spain, and that she's a painter and an art historian. Surprisingly, in that web page you can see some of her paintings with frames, just like the ones we have at home but larger! To make a long story short, she came over and we talked for a long time. She's a lovely woman, very educated and proper. She said she bought her frames in Granada, Spain, where there are still artisans that do that kind of work, which is very old and comes from Syria. She looked at the pictures of the other bargueños and told us that she'd like to see them. If it was okay with us, she herself would drive us in her car back home tomorrow, if possible. I said yes, of course, but that we couldn't make any decisions because we had to wait to see what kind of offer Museo del Virreinato would make us. She said that was fine, she understood and would pick us up early in the morning. I already told your dad to be ready.

The air conditioner suddenly kicked in and blew cold air on Adriana's face; one of the vents was directly above her. Esperanza let out a soft moan and rolled over in the bed. She was still asleep, and another soft moan turned into a snore. Adriana turned off the air conditioner with the remote control on the bedside table. The light coming through the half-open curtain was enough to locate it. She was happy and surprised with her mom's message. She'd imagined that it would be her father who'd take care of everything. Her mother always played a second fiddle in whatever concerned their family or their home. Perhaps it was the good influence of Cousin Carmen who was a more modern, liberated woman.

Before leaving the museum, her mother went on, *we saw the bargueños they have on display. Cousin Carmen and I were stunned. Bewildered! They have two large sixteenth-century bargueños with tables that are identical to the ones Grandfather Rafael was hiding in the storage room. One of them had a long caption next to it. It said it was the bargueño that appeared in the movie, The Mission, in a scene at the Episcopal Palace in Cartagena. Do you remember that we watched that movie at home and Grandpa Rafael was furious when we got to that scene? Remember he made us rewind the tape and watch the scene again, and then he said that it was impossible? The poor old man. We thought he'd gone crazy and was talking about the Cardinal in the movie. The caption also said that a magazine had published a story about that bargueño because it belonged to someone important; a relative of one of the Spanish Viceroys in Bogotá. Good thing we didn't throw it away! The old man, may he rest in peace, had them reserved for you, Adriana. We never imagined that the old man had made covers to close them up permanently. Were it not for the letters the old man left us and those he sent you in Japan, we would've never known what he'd done. I'm sending you some pictures. How exciting that you're getting them right away. I've told your dad to buy a new computer to have internet and send you letters and photos any time we want, but you know how he is; he says it's a luxury we can't afford, that the phone is enough—as long as it's you who pays for the long-distance calls!*

Adriana scrolled the text down to the end of the message and saw that there were indeed several photos, which she opened immediately. One of them was a selfie of her mother with her Cousin Carmen at the entrance of the Museo del Virreinato. How cute her mom looked! She was well-groomed with a new hairstyle and was wearing makeup. Adriana felt again that she was going to cry, but this time she choked it back.

She heard the roar of an engine outside and opened the curtain a sliver. There was a line of cars by the hotel entrance picking people up, maybe from the bar. The neon light that now bathed the room came from of a supermarket across the street, which was apparently open twenty-four hours a day. There were people coming and going as if they were in broad daylight. She closed the curtain. She was not in the mood to take in the early morning scene; it reminded her of Roppongi, of a past she wanted to forget.

She looked back at the selfie. Cousin Carmen also looked good and was dressed in designer clothes. That part of the family were very well-off people; they lived in a nice house that was in a fancy neighborhood. The other photos were of the bargueños in the San Benito storage room at home. The largest one that her grandfather had made a cover for looked to be in perfect shape. All the engravings and pieces of marquetry were in place.

How much money could they get for them all? Her father had tried to sell them to one of the wealthy landowners in town, but he'd offered him peanuts. Maybe he didn't believe they were real antiques, or more likely, he was trying to cheat him. Rich people were always like that. It was how they made their money, always taking it from the poor.

On the last paragraph, her mother had written that she was very happy that she was with Esperanza, and that she was a very enterprising girl. It was a blessing from heaven that her father had taught her bookkeeping, and now that she knew how the world was and how it went round, she should be careful and wise and do the best she could. Adriana felt tears on her cheeks again and bit her lip.

FIVE

When Tony arrived at Carlos Santana's show at the Dubai Jazz Festival, he realized that he misread the information about it in the weekly city guide. Or rather read it hastily and did not notice that it was the last number of the evening, and he would have to wait almost two hours. He read the brochure that they gave him at the entrance and learned that there were three presentations before the final show; two groups from the U.S., winners of some prizes he'd never heard of, and a British band led by a London-based bassist who played weekend gigs at a luxury beach hotel in Dubai during the winter season. How clumsy he'd been, he thought. He could have had a relaxing dinner and a glass of wine instead of eating a sandwich he'd made on the fly, which may later give him heartburn.

The night had turned a bit cold and windy. The moonless sky was full of stars, and there were no electric lights around other than on the street the taxi had taken that was two or three kilometers from a shopping mall by the creek on the edge of the city. The venue was on flat ground bordered by bushes and next to a golf course. The concert stage was at the far end, framed by large speakers and stage lights. In front of it, there were rows of chairs. The first three or four were already taken by middle-aged Europeans and North Americans as far as he could see. In the back, marking the perimeter, there was a two-level wooden hut lined with advertisements for a Caribbean rum. In the lower part there was a bar, and in the upper section, a platform with armchairs and sofas that could be the VIP area where, according to the advertisement for the show, the tickets were five times more expensive than his. He thought that maybe it would be worth paying the extra money. He would be more comfortable, could have a few drinks, and enjoy the show, which he was sure would bring him many memories. Santana was one of his favorite musicians.

Just then, a group of tall young women came out from behind the structure wearing tight dresses, like promotional models at motorsport events. He pulled his binoculars out of his backpack and watched the group; they looked Russian or Eastern European. Perhaps it was not a good idea to go as he might be tempted to flirt. One of them, the only one without high heels, was talking on her mobile. She seemed annoyed. She put a hand on her forehead, like someone who had just heard bad news, and took a few hurried steps in his direction. As she drew closer, he realized it was Wendy who he had not seen in a month or so. Did someone alert her that he was watching with binoculars?

Tony raised his hand to say hi, but she didn't return the greeting. Perhaps she didn't recognize him.

"Sorry, I didn't see you," Wendy said and shook his hand. That evening, Wendy was wearing makeup, which made her look younger though also somewhat generic, like the other women in the group.

Tony told her not to worry, that the lighting was not very good back there, and asked her how she was and why she had not gone back to the Sonatine.

"I've been traveling," she replied a little flustered. "Also, I moved apartments," she added. "I now live near here. Although, to be frank, I miss the old neighborhood."

"It's the first time I've come to this city-within-the-city," Tony said. "I didn't even know it existed."

"It is a bit isolated from the rest of the city, although it is near everything. The international airport is very close, and we are right on the creek. How is it going at work?"

"Everything's fine," Tony replied and looked Wendy in the eye. He thought he saw a glint of mischief in them.

"Are you working?" he asked.

"Yes, I'm a consultant to the event organizers," Wendy replied. "Tonight, I'm giving them a hand with the VIP area."

"Did you quit your work at the university?"

"No, not at all," Wendy said and smiled. "It's a second job, only part-time, and it's occasional. I mean seasonal, mostly in the winter. Did you come to see Santana?"

"Yes, but I came too early. I didn't read the small print on the ad!"

"You could come to our box and have a drink until the show starts. Don't worry about a ticket. I'll give you a complimentary VIP pass. What do you say?"

"It'd be a pleasure. Thanks," Tony replied.

Wendy took him upstairs and asked him to sit in one of the leather armchairs by the corner. She told him she would be back in ten or fifteen minutes, and that he should get comfortable and enjoy the welcome cocktail that someone would bring him in a few minutes.

He thanked her again and told her that he was really glad to see her. He immediately regretted it; he felt that he had somehow exposed himself with his words.

Wendy nodded her head, and hurriedly went downstairs.

From his armchair, Tony had a panoramic view. Beyond the stage, he could see the creek and the contour of the city in the distance, and to his left, a golf course with an imposing well-lit clubhouse in the shape of a Bedouin desert tent. He thought it was an extraordinary coincidence to see Wendy again. Professor Deenik had not mentioned her the few times they had chatted on the street corner across from Café Sonatine where he always went to watch the sunset with his terrier. He had assumed that she had left the country for good.

He had been a little depressed of late; the routine and silence of his exile was taking its toll. During the last month, he had imposed on himself a rigid schedule of work, reading, and exercise to fill the hours in the city where he felt like a refugee; displaced and forgotten. In the morning, he read his Japanese novels with his dictionaries at hand, taking note of every *kanji* character he didn't know. In the afternoon, he applied a similarly rigor to Sonatine's accounting books; he noted all the errors and inconsistencies in a notebook in an effort to figure out the money laundering scheme that Vladimir's Russian friends used.

Once they served his cocktail, a *mojito* in a tall glass, he checked his email in his mobile, but he only found spam messages from a dating service. He was waiting for news from Vladimir, who wrote to him the week before to tell him that things in Roppongi had taken an unexpected turn that required a change of plans; a postponement of his return to work. On the other hand, a couple of days ago, his friend Pablo, the Peruvian journalist, told him that a special unit of the Police was investigating the disappearance of Adriana, something that was out of the ordinary. Perhaps someone important was behind that. Perhaps the same Colombian ambassador who was said to be a man who advocated for the rights of sex workers. What surprised him was that Vladimir had not mentioned anything about what the bosses had decided about Adriana's debt, whether it was up to him to pay it or not, and how much it would be. The silence was worrisome because it could mean that they had decided to keep him out of the business, which would mean that he would owe them money and could not return to work with them.

Wendy returned a few minutes later when they began to set up the microphones for the first set. With her came a slender young man, about twenty-five years old, sporting a carefully shaved goatee and casually dressed in jeans and a brand name polo shirt. She introduced him as her friend, Fardan Al Fardan, a fourth-year student at the university. They sat on the sofa that was diagonal to him.

The young man said that it was a pleasure for him to meet one of Wendy's friends, and asked him what he was doing in Dubai. Tony told him about Café Sonatine, and Fardan said he knew the place and had gone several times to buy a carrot cake that his girlfriend liked. Fardan spoke English with a British accent and smiled when enunciating the words with some affectation as if he were acting in front of cameras.

Wendy laughed and said that Fardan had many girlfriends, but the one he was referring to wasn't really his girlfriend, but a young woman he had a crush on.

"Wendy is very mean to me," Fardan said and raised his eyebrows. "She knows very well that I am madly in love with one of her friends, a very attractive Spaniard. Are you Spanish?"

"My roots are South American," Tony said.

"Fardan says he can guess people's nationality in less than five minutes," Wendy remarked.

South Americans always confuse me: there are some like you who could very well be Spanish, but also Lebanese or Syrian, Fardan hastened to explain.

"If you'd said Syrian, you would have partially guessed," Tony said. "In my family, there is Syrian blood from several generations ago."

"I'm not surprised," said Fardan. "Some time ago, I read something about Arab migration to the Americas. If I remember correctly, there are very prominent people of Arab descent in those countries. Millionaires, presidents, and artists like Shakira. Do you know what tribe or family your relatives descended from?"

"I don't know much about that branch of my family. They are from the Caribbean region. My parents are from the central region, from the capital. The only thing I know for sure is that those distant relatives were Christians, and that they arrived in Colombia in the late nineteenth century carrying Turkish passports. But that was a long time ago and no one from that branch of the family has a connection with Syria now, or much less knows the Arabic language or culture, apart from some cooking recipes which they still use. My maternal grandfather went to Damascus once to a family reunion in the nineteen fifties; we had some pictures from that time, but a few years after his return he married my grandmother who was not of Arab origin. In fact, she was of Portuguese-Jewish origin, and they went to live in the capital."

While Tony was speaking, Fardan stroked his goatee as if meditating on something. "It's a pity that they lost their original identity," he said and left the sentence up in the air.

"In any case," he added, "I need to know more South Americans. I think there are not many of you in Dubai."

"There are enough for a party at a concert hall," said Wendy.

"A party? What kind of party?" Tony asked.

"I don't know," Wendy replied and frowned. "I think it's a private event, by invitation only."

"The event you told me about?" Fardan asked.

"Right," Wendy replied. "Your beloved is there right now, a work thing, in case you want to know. She gave us a hand tonight, by the way."

"Did someone not come?" Fardan asked.

"Yes, two of the hostesses were ill, or so they told me this afternoon. Their replacements arrived a few minutes ago. They said that the taxi driver who brought them got lost, and took them to the other side of the golf course."

Fardan made a face of surprise, he told them to excuse him for a moment and called someone on his mobile. Smiling as he had done so far, he began to speak in Arabic. Tony looked again at his mailbox on his own mobile, but there was still no message from Vladimir. Wendy did the same, maybe she was also expecting a message or to hear from someone.

"The signs on the streets during the festival have always been a problem," said Fardan when he finished his call. "But taxi drivers are also to blame," he added and shook his finger as if blaming someone. "They rarely follow street signs. They only rely on what they tell each other on the phone.

"They're also overworked," Wendy interrupted.

"Wendy is right," Fardan said and crossed his arms. "The real problem are the signs though," he added.

"Fardan's family owns the company that built this city-within-the-city," Wendy said in a conciliatory tone.

"It's a joint venture with a British construction company," Fardan explained. "There are also investors from other countries, Americans too; as you can see, the three hotels next to the mall are from U.S. chains."

"It looks quite fancy around here. Is it an Emirati neighborhood?" Tony asked.

"Not really," Fardan answered and looked at Wendy out of the corner of his eye. "We Emiratis usually live in bigger houses. We have big families, you know. Around here the tenants are usually expat; Europeans, Americans, and some Arabs and Indians too.

"Only renters? Isn't it possible to buy property here?"

Fardan raised his eyes and settled back in his chair. He had yet another mobile in his jean pockets, which he placed over the one he'd just used on the table. "The board of directors recently decided that they were going to sell to foreigners," he said. "It would be necessary to create a freehold area. The lawyers are working on that, but it will take a few months. We have some luxury properties overlooking the creek, which I think will sell very well and very fast; many people want to invest in our country."

For some reason, Tony thought of his Japanese boss, the main shareholder of the Roppongi clubs from whom he expected news. He had once told him that the best real estate investments were in tax havens like Dubai.

"Can a foreign company buy property here?" he asked.

Fardan again arched his eyebrows. "Not at the moment," he acknowledged. "The lawyers are also working on that. If you are interested, you should stop by our office; it's very close from here."

"I'm just curious. I'm far from being an investor. I asked because I read something about it in one of the local newspapers."

"I see," Fardan said, looking quickly at one of his mobiles that had just vibrated. "I don't want to bore you with business talk," he added in a cheerful tone and switched off the mobile that had vibrated. Perhaps it was a business line and he was really not in the mood. "Why don't we talk about music? Is jazz popular in your country?"

"You read my mind, Fardan," Wendy said. "I was going to ask Tony exactly that."

"Yes, of course," Tony replied and put a hand on his chin. "But I left Colombia a while ago, so I'm not up to speed with the jazz scene over there." He was going to tell them a story about some Colombian friends who once owned a jazz club in Bogotá, and were now working in Tokyo, but he suddenly felt that he shouldn't volunteer any information that betrayed his business connections. Fardan and Wendy, who perhaps noticed that he'd changed his mind, looked at each other for a moment.

"What I find interesting," Fardan said and lit a cigarette, "is that the organizers—all British, by the way—selected Santana as the most important event for this year's festival. But Santana is Latin Pop, don't you think?"

"Santana has done a lot of music, including Pop, but his earlier work in the nineteen-seventies was Rock or Latin Rock, which in his style was definitely also Jazz, Latin Jazz," Tony said.

"Santana in the seventies!" Fardan exclaimed. "I didn't know he was so old; he would be my grandfather's age then."

Wendy laughed and said, "one of the courses that should be included in the university's curriculum should cover the history of popular music in the world."

"It's not a bad idea," Fardan said and flashed a fake smile. "Our Provost will have a fit when I tell him about this," he added, and he and Wendy burst out laughing.

"My apologies," Wendy said and looked at Tony. "It's an inside joke for those who know the university. You can't imagine what kind of place it is!"

The musicians who were set to play the first set, a British group, had already settled in. From the stage came the first bars of *You Shook Me Baby*, a well-known blues song by Muddy Waters.

"I think the organizers of the event know very well what they're doing," Tony said.

"It would have been best if they had invited Led Zeppelin," Wendy added and winked at Tony.

"You know Led Zeppelin?" It was now Tony who took the lead addressing Fardan.

"They are Heavy Metal, right?"

"Yes, you could say that. But just as in the case of Santana, they did other things too. Led Zeppelin adapted this song to their style of Rock, but if you pay attention, it's still Blues, which some would argue is also Jazz."

"I think we need that kind of History class," Fardan said and turned his attention to the guitar solo that had started.

The cocktail was quite strong, perhaps they had put a double shot of Rum. Tony felt transported by the music. It was one of his favorite songs. It reminded him of his days as a college student in New York when he lived with his first serious girlfriend, who was from Japan and was doing a degree in graphic design. They rented an apartment in Astoria overlooking the East River and spent many hours listening to music and smoking weed. It was a happy time, but it did not last long. Two years or so. As soon as she finished her degree, she went to Boston to graduate school, and they never saw each other again.

At some point, Fardan raised his hand as if greeting someone who had just arrived. Coming up the stairs were two young men dressed in white *dishdasha*, the traditional Emirati-style tunic, and behind them, one of the promotional models, a tall Slavic-looking blonde.

"It was nice to meet you," Fardan said and offered Tony his hand as he stood up. "I'm sure we'll meet again. If you need anything, don't hesitate to call me," he added and gave him a business card. Fardan waved goodbye to Wendy and shook hands with the newcomers. He kissed the blonde on both cheeks and took her by the hand to the other side of the box. The young Emiratis sat on armchairs in front of them, facing the stage, and in a moment, two of the other promotional models came to attend to them.

SIX

A cramp suddenly woke him up. It was a sharp and un-
bearable pain, like a high-voltage current probe slithering
through his leg and into his calf. As if by reflex, Tony quickly
sat up on the bed, took his foot in his hands and extended
his leg as much as he could. He refrained from making any
noise. He didn't want to awaken Wendy, who was sleeping
next to him. The cramp subsided a little but didn't fade, and
he had to repeat the maneuver twice more. He lay down
again and felt exhausted. His throat was dry. He looked at
the night table next to him. He thought maybe there would
be a glass of water, but there was nothing but a small reading lamp. He remembered that everything had happened
quickly after Santana's show ended at the jazz festival. Wendy asked him for a drink at her place, and when they arrived,
she took him by the hand directly to her bed, then told him
that she wanted to make love and started to undress.

A few seconds after the third stretch, he felt that his calf
had relaxed. From the bathroom, next to the bed on his side,
came a soft beam of light that was perhaps from the night

light. He was fully awake and realized he was wearing something that wasn't his. He touched the fabric and remembered that it was an oversized t-shirt that Wendy lent him after they were done making love. He also remembered that before she turned the lights off, she told him goodnight, sleep well, and kissed him on the cheek, which had felt odd. Both the words and the kiss were odd, and for an instant he felt out of place and unsettled. He must have dozed off right away. Something that seldom happened to him as he usually had trouble falling asleep. Perhaps exhaustion had set in. Their lovemaking had been intense. He had not had sex since the last time with Adriana months ago, which a distant memory now. He thought that Wendy was very much like him, or so a female version of him. She did what he would have done with no pauses or preludes. She went straight to the point and got what she wanted. Then, though it may not have been her intention, she made it clear that it would be she who would take the lead in whatever it was that was happening. This included being the first one to say good night and sleep well.

He got up and went for a glass of water. There was a short corridor that led to the open kitchen, which overlooked the living room. There was no need to turn any of the lamps on. The glow of the city in the distance came through the floor to ceiling windows and bathed his surroundings with a faint light. Wendy's apartment had the same generic air as his own, though the furnishings were of better quality as well as the building as a whole. They were on the tenth floor, facing the creek, which extended beyond his field of vision. Two bridges crossed it at each side. Both were lit neon blue along the sides. The traffic on them looked light but steady. The marks of a city that never sleeps. The sky was clear with the exception of large chunks of whitish clouds hovering over the city beyond. A Dhow, a wooden merchant ship, sailed under the bridge to his right towards the mouth of the creek and the open sea. There were no lights anywhere on it, except for a red dot on of the bow. It looked like a ghost ship. On the other side of the creek, there were several luxury yachts berthed in the marina of an elegant European style building that was six or seven stories high with arched windows. Perhaps it was a hotel; he could see a swimming pool and a sunbathing area and several gardens with palm trees and ornamental shrubbery.

After drinking a few sips of water, he walked into the living room and took his binoculars out of his backpack on the sofa. He wanted to find his building, or at least his neighborhood, which was on the other side of the creek, a few kilometers away. There were several construction cranes that obstructed the view, but in the distance, he could see the hotel that was near the Bank Street intersection. That was where Wendy told him the Latin party was, right across from where he had seen her that other night when he followed her. He had passed by the building several times, always during the day, and had not noticed that the place advertised itself as a concert hall. Wendy said it was a big place and accommodated at least two hundred people. It would have been interesting to go to that party. He would have found a discreet, dark spot where he could've watched without being seen.

On one of the living room walls, there were several bookcases. Tony took a quick look, the faint light from outside was enough to see the spines of some of the books, which were mostly literature; collections of British and American authors, also some Japanese. On top of the bookcases, were several framed photographs that were all of Wendy with other people, probably colleagues and friends. On one of them was taken outside a university in Tokyo in a part of the city that he knew well, not far from Roppongi. Wendy was next to a man who at that moment was looking to one side, and his face was not visible. Perhaps it was a picture taken in a hurry, or that man did not want to be photographed. Two or three blocks away was the language school where he taught English for a few weeks after he'd arrived in Japan. The owner had hired him on the condition that he use another name; he'd told him that in general Japanese students preferred Anglo-Saxon teachers. He had accepted and from that day on he'd introduced himself as Tony Morray, a native of Lackawanna, a town in upstate New York, which inevitably elicited laughter in class.

The photograph next to it attracted his attention even more. It was a beach scene where Wendy appeared next to Fardan, though…was it Fardan? No, it wasn't him. It took him a moment to realize, although the resemblance was remarkable. It was someone older, about forty-five years old or so. It would have to be a close relative, an older brother, or an uncle, or perhaps his father. Judging from the lush landscape and the thatched roofs in the background, it was probably in South East Asia where he had backpacked years ago.

He thought Wendy was full of surprises. Perhaps she had, as he had always had, a double life in every sense of the word. In addition to her work at the university, she was an events consultant, which, from what he had seen tonight and the night of the crash, included managing, maybe also hiring, models and hostesses who could very well have other duties or obligations. How much this consulting was like what he and Adriana did in Tokyo was something he had to find out. Perhaps, if he was not allowed to return to work in Tokyo, he could manage to stay in Dubai and become an events consultant like Wendy, or maybe become in partnership with her. Wendy was not Adriana, but if what he suspected was true, she was *like* Adriana. They both kept secrets, and he needed to know them. He sensed that they would be useful to him, and that they would benefit him in some way.

He leaned back on the sofa and watched the clouds in the sky, which were now scattered like a herd of sheep, running away into the horizon. He felt peaceful, and at the same time invigorated. He was sure he would sleep well from now on. It was an instinctive but absolute certainty.

SEVEN

There was a traffic jam on Sheikh Zayed Road due to an accident; a bus from a construction company had crashed into the concrete barrier and overturned. The vehicle lay diagonally to the barrier and occupied two lanes that were now closed as several police cars were blocking it. There was no sign that anyone had been injured, perhaps they had already taken them away. You could hear the wailing siren of an ambulance in the distance.

Paola and Esperanza were on their way to meet Tomás Rodrigues, a Colombian professor at a university in Dubai who had published an article about colonial furniture in Colombia. He might be able to give further information about the bargueños that Paola had inherited from her Grandfather Rafael. Esperanza had contacted him through an Australian friend who was into antiques and worked at the university's library.

Paola felt tired and a little edgy. In the last few days, she had to help Esperanza manage hostesses and models at a conference on public administration in the Arab World. The work was exhausting because they had to attend meetings and ceremonies, greet dignitaries and participate in photo shoots with them, as well as accompany them to social functions. Besides, she had not slept well the night before either. Something had suddenly woken her up at dawn; a noise or a thump coming from the apartment above, and then she had sunk into a series of fitful dreams that went on for far too long. The scenes were in a jungle and a river that she ended up forgetting immediately after she woke up.

Professor Rodrigues was typing something on his computer when they arrived at the cafe at a themed shopping mall that commemorated the voyages of the great Moroccan Berber, Ibn Battuta, along the southern highway towards Abu Dhabi. He looked just like the picture on the university's website; middle-aged and bald with a salt and pepper goatee. He wore a black shirt with a Chinese collar and white linen pants, which Paola thought gave him an air of a soap opera patriarch.

"Thank you for coming from the other side of the city, professor, and please forgive us for being so late," she said and shook his hand. "If you don't have much time, we could drive you home and we could talk in the car, would that be all right?"

Rodrigues looked at his watch and said yes, that it was a good idea. It suited him because the metro station was far from his home. "But I'm not really in a hurry," he said and smiled from ear to ear. "How about we get something to drink first and chat for a while before leaving?"

"As you wish," Paola said and looked at Esperanza who nodded yes. "Did you have any trouble finding this place, professor?"

"Your directions were very clear," Rodrigues replied. "From the metro station, you reach the Egyptian court at the end of which there is a long corridor that leads to the Andalusian court, and in the middle there is a fountain of lions, a replica of the one at the famous palace of the Alhambra, across from which is this Starbucks. You go from one continent to another, from antiquity to the twelfth century, and then on to the twenty-first century in the blink of an eye."

"That's right, professor. This city is full of surprises, don't you think?" Esperanza intervened. "You haven't been here long, have you? In your email, you said you were a visiting professor, right?"

"For a year, although I have the option of extending the contract for another year," Rodrigues replied and crossed his arms.

"I get the sense that you've been away from Colombia for a long time. I can't place your accent," Paola said and coughed a little; her throat was dry.

"I'm from Bogotá, but I guess I've lost my accent over the years. I've spent more than half of my life out of Colombia. I studied in Australia and then..." Rodrigues was going to continue, but at that moment the waitress arrived to take their order. On the other side of the cafe across from them, a group of young women wearing colorful hijabs were talking loudly and clapping, perhaps in celebration of some achievement or special event.

"How can I help you?" Rodrigues asked when the waitress left and the clapping subsided. "I was very intrigued with the news that you had in your possession two bargueños from the colonial period. I had to re-read that old article I wrote about colonial museums in Colombia. I couldn't remember the particulars."

"My grandfather left them to me as an inheritance," Paola said. "The old man had kept them, hidden rather, in the San Benito room of our house. Fortunately, before he died, he told dad they were authentic antiques, an inheritance from his own father, and made him promise to get expert advice for their sale. The problem," she added with emphasis, "is that the curators at the Museo del Virreinato in Bogotá, whom we commissioned to make an appraisal, are telling us that they need to make a more detailed study and that we would have to wait for at least two months. This is a problem for us because we urgently need to sell them to cover some unexpected expenses at home."

"But did they tell you anything? Did they say something specifically?" Rodrigues asked.

"They said they were sure they are authentic pieces from that period," Paola replied. And, that they are the work of a Spanish or a Creole artisan, in any case, a master. But that it was a *complex* case."

"In what sense complex?" Rodrigues asked and narrowed his eyes.

"We asked them what was missing, and they answered that it was a matter of historical evidence, that they needed to consult some archives in Bogotá."

"And Professor Cortés could not help you?"

"No, professor," Paola replied. "He told us that you were the only person he knew who could help us."

"I see," Rodrigues said and stroked his goatee. "I haven't heard from him for a long time. He helped me a lot with my undergraduate thesis. He's retired now, isn't he?"

"At a Jesuit retirement home in Bogotá," Paola said. "My mom went to visit him there and chatted with him."

"I see. A Jesuit to the very end. We didn't get along very well, but I admired him. I admired him very much. May I see the photos?"

Paola nodded and took out her mobile, looked for the files, and handed it to Rodrigues.

He looked at the pictures intently and furrowed his brow. "At first sight, it looks identical to the one they have at the Museum del Virreinato," he said. "The famous *Arca de Noé* bargueño. I now understand why the curators said they needed more time.

"Do you see the engraving in the center?" he asked and put the phone on the table. He had enlarged the photo of the front of the large bargueño.

"A bearded man wearing a turban," Paola said.

"That's not a turban," Esperanza objected. "If you look closely, what he's wearing is a crown. I think it's an image of Christ the King. At home, we had an image in the same style."

Paola pulled her chair closer and looked carefully at the engraving. Seen up close, the way Esperanza, who was next to Rodrigues, was looking at it, some of the vertical imperfections in the bone plate that had been darkened by time added to the pattern of the turban and gave it a more rigid appearance, perhaps like a crown, but also like some sort of helmet. Looking from afar it was undoubtedly a turban. The image of Christ the King was Esperanza's wishful thinking, she thought. She had always been somewhat religious. She went to a Catholic school run by nuns, and still went to church on Sundays; very much the opposite of her who had gone to public schools and scarcely remembered how to pray. The image of her Grandfather Rafael came to mind. He used to say that religious images were deceptive and that people should not pray to them unless they understood what they really meant, something that irritated her mother who would mutter under her breath that the old man was crazy.

"If it's a man with a turban, it could be Maimonides, a famous Jewish medieval philosopher," Rodrigues said. "In that case, that bargueño could be the original; the one the museum *claims* to have. The one they have on display is probably a twin, that is, one of a pair that the owners commissioned to be made, although perhaps not at the same time."

"If the one we have is the original *Arca de Noé*, would it be more valuable than the one they have in the museum?" Paola asked and looked at Esperanza, who had wrinkled her forehead slightly as if she didn't agree with her asking that question to Rodrigues. That morning Esperanza had told her that they had to proceed with caution. That Rodrigues could help them understand the *value* of the bargueño, but for its actual *worth* in money, they should consult with someone knowledgeable of the antique business. She added that she knew someone who could help them with that. A British client of hers who worked with a well-known auction house that had a branch office in Dubai.

"Yes, much more valuable, but I can't think of how much in dollars and cents," Rodrigues said and scratched his temple. "To tell you the truth, I don't know how you can assign a price to an object like that. This bargueño can help us to better understand the history of that period."

"But there would be no problem selling it, right?" That the bargueño was very valuable was what Paola wanted to hear, but what Rodrigues said about understanding the history of the period didn't sound good to her; it was like the forecast of a storm.

"No, I don't think so," said Rodrigues. "If it's indeed the original, the museum would want to have it. I think they would pay very well, I have no doubt…" Rodrigues made as if he was going to add something else but left the sentence in the air and looked Paola in the eye as if he had realized something but was hesitant to say it.

"Then the bargueño that appears in *The Mission*, the

movie, is a copy of the twin, not of the original." Esperanza interrupted in a hurried tone and looked at Paola out of the corner of her eye, perhaps as a hint that this was the course the conversation should follow.

"Yes, I suppose so," Rodrigues replied in his normal tone of voice, his gaze now on Esperanza. "The producers of the film commissioned some artisans—I don't know whether in Colombia or in Spain—to make a copy of it so they could use it in some important scenes, like when the Cardinal decides on the fate of the Jesuit missions. But regarding what you just said," he went on, "I would say that the two, I mean the three, are originals. Those pieces are not easy to make; they require specialized knowledge of designs, techniques, and materials. If the one you have is the original, in the chronological sense—the one that was made first—then the one that is in the museum, which might have been originally made to be its twin, is also an original—though not the *Arca de Noé*—because it has a different engraving in the central panel, which gives it a different meaning. As long as the museum has done the appropriate tests to authenticate its age, of course. It is possible to fake old age in wooden furniture; I mean to pass a new piece of furniture for an old one. It is not easy, but it is possible. People who work on restorations know how to do it."

"And why do you think that what we have is the original?" Paola asked.

"Because there are some historical documents that suggest it," Rodrigues replied. "It would be necessary to investigate thoroughly, of course," he added.

"What documents?" Paola and Esperanza asked almost at the same time.

"It's a long story, but I'll make it short," Rodrigues said. "The bargueño they have in the Museo del Virreinato was a gift that the museum received from a family in Bogotá when they opened their doors more than eighty years ago. At that time, they didn't have the authentication and documentation systems that they do now, so it was cataloged as *Arca de Noé* as per the instructions of the Ruiz Valenzuela family that gifted it. Many years later, in the nineteen-nineties, Professor Cortés discovered in a nineteenth-century judicial file an inventory of the furnishings of a Bogotá businessman who filed for bankruptcy. It listed a valuable bargueño, known as *Arca de Noé*, whose description is like the one they have in the museum except for the central engraving which shows San Francis of Assisi, but that the inventory document describes as depicting 'an important figure of his faith'."

"Maimonides the Jewish philosopher?" Paola asked.

"That was what Professor Cortés concluded at that time," Rodrigues replied and drummed his fingers on the table. "Some of the descendants of that businessman that Professor Cortés interviewed claimed they were of Jewish ancestry, though they didn't have any documentation to prove it. But that is not surprising. Jewish lineage wasn't always something you'd want people to know. The Jews were expelled from Spain by the Catholic Kings in the fifteen Century, and many who made it to the Americas were prosecuted by the Inquisition until the eighteen hundredths. As you can imagine, many hid their identity, even destroyed documents and any other evidence of Jewish ancestry."

Rodrigues said this last in a brooding tone, as if to himself, and drank the rest of the mineral water that was in his glass. "Things have changed, of course," he continued, his voice now a little louder. "The Spanish government has recently promised to bestow citizenship to all those who prove to be descendants of Jews expelled from Spain. The case of this family is complicated, but it is likely that they descend from Jews who converted to Catholicism and arrived in the New World in the sixteenth century."

Rodrigues paused and looked at the lion fountain next to the cafe as if meditating on something. "It may be better if we continue with the issue on the way," he said after a few moments. He arched his eyes as if it were a question.

While walking to the parking lot, Paola thought that in Bogotá things could get complicated if the curators at the museum confirmed that the bargueño her grandfather had left her was the original *Arca de Noé*. The museum could claim that it belonged to them, or that it belonged to the country, or that it was part of the nation's cultural heritage, or something like that. Anything could happen in Colombia! Or they might suggest—it occurred to her almost in a panic—that Grandfather Rafael had stolen it. That was absurd, though. Her grandfather was no thief! He had always been a very honest man. He didn't owe anything to anybody, nor had he gotten into any trouble with anyone—as far as she knew. Her father always said that her grandfather was a very straight arrow. Although, he also criticized him because he was stingy. The old man is a *Jew*, his father had said many times, she suddenly remembered. But that had been a joke. Or not? Could her grandfather have been truly Jewish? Most likely not, but she would have to ask.

EIGHT

Professor Rodrigues' apartment was on a high floor in a residential tower in the Marina District. The living and dining room had a sea view, although the only thing you could see at the moment was a jumble of sand-laden clouds that covered the horizon. Outside, there was a rough disorderly wind that made the sliding door to the balcony whistle. The palm trees on the sidewalk in front of the building swayed with the wind, and on the street bits and pieces of shrubbery and debris rolled every which way with a few plastic bags abruptly rising like balloons flying with the wind. The sandstorm had started without warning as they were on the highway on their way back to the city just when they were about to take the exit towards Professor Rodrigues' neighborhood.

"Thanks for giving us shelter," Paola said and sat on the sofa next to Esperanza, who was looking for something in her purse. Maybe her compact mirror to touch up her makeup, which was something that she did every chance she had, it was second nature to her.

"Not at all, you're very welcome," Rodrigues replied from

the kitchen that opened into the dining room in a manner that increasingly made him sound as if he were from the well-off northern neighborhoods of Bogotá. At some point during the trip he had begun to talk like that, perhaps because it was the manner and tone he adopted in the company of other Colombians, a way of blending in. Or maybe because it was part of his true nature, what he had learned as a child but that had been dissipating over time. Whatever it was, it was a tone that Paola detested. It brought back unpleasant memories of her life in Bogotá as a student from the provinces; of the times her classmates made fun of her way of speaking and also of her jokes, even of the way she laughed. At home in her town, it was what endeared her to her parents and friends.

"It's a *gorgeous* apartment, professor," Esperanza said in a way that echoed the professor's tone, tinged with the flirty manner she had with some men. Paola thought that perhaps they liked each other, and what she was witnessing was a kind of courtship. Although, it was more likely the beginning of an infatuation for Esperanza, who fell very easily in love with a certain type of man, usually professional, wealthy, and European-looking. Especially if she described him as *sophisticated*, a quality that she determined variously. It could be in reference to the clothes he wore or the car he drove, for example, even the type of cocktail he ordered at the bar, depending on the circumstances.

"I was lucky the university gave me this apartment," Rodrigues said as he entered the room with a tray with glasses of lemonade that he left on the coffee table where he had some books on Islamic architecture. "It was fully furnished," he continued and motioned them to take their drinks. "The only thing I did was shift the desk to the living room, which as you can see is quite big, and has a sea view. Now invisible, of course."

"Well, I think it is *so* you, professor," Esperanza said and smiled in a way that Paola thought fit for a television commercial.

"You left us very intrigued with your story," Paola interjected, and cleared her throat. "Would you mind telling us the rest?"

"Of course," Rodrigues replied, and looked at the sandstorm which seemed to darken the sky by the minute. During the trip home, Esperanza had asked him to tell them what had brought him to Dubai, and Rodrigues, who answered that it was something related to his work but also because of a personal matter, little by little started to tell them about something that had happened to him in the past that had left them intrigued. It was about a love affair that he had over a period of several years with a Dutch woman of Asian roots. He had met her when he was on his way to Australia to do his graduate degree, with whom he unfortunately broke up with and never saw again because of a misunderstanding. It started on a passenger ferry that crossed the Malacca Strait between Malaysia and the Indonesian island of Sumatra where they met; continued on over several months of backpacking throughout the Indonesian archipelago; and then over a period of two years in Sydney, Australia, where they lived together until the young woman, whose name was Monica, had to return to Indonesia to continue with a research project she had undertaken in order to get her degree in Anthropology.

At first, Paola thought Rodrigues had made up the story. Some of the things he told them seemed, to her, implausible, as if taken from a novel or a movie. She could not imagine the soft-spoken Rodrigues, who seemed to her like a priest rather than a professor, going on a backpacking trip in an Asian country and falling head over heels with the hippie girl he had described. But as Rodrigues went on telling his story, she realized that there was no artifice in it. He told it with conviction and emotion, as if it were happening to him right then and there. The intriguing part, and perhaps the one that made her change her mind, was when Rodrigues told them that many years later on a trip to India, he had seen a young woman who looked so much like Monica she could have been her double, a doppelgänger. At that moment, Paola turned around to look at Rodrigues, who was sitting in the back seat, and noticed in his face a grimace of anguish, as if he was still grappling with the strange encounter.

Paola asked him what had happened, and Rodrigues replied that it had been a very strong shock because of the memories that had come to him, though not it did not compare and was not as dramatic as what had happened later when he found out that the young woman, whose name was Miryam, was Monica's daughter. Esperanza, who perhaps had also noticed Rodrigues' reaction in the rearview mirror, asked him if that young woman was his daughter. Rodrigues told her that Monica, who had died of cancer a few years ago, had written in her diary that the young woman's father was an Indian doctor of Portuguese origin, from Goa whom she had met in Indonesia. He was about to continue with his story, but at that point they had to exit the highway, and he had to give directions for Esperanza to get to his building.

Rodrigues nodded his head and rubbed his goatee before speaking. "As I told you on our way here," Rodrigues went on in a slow and confidential tone, "Monica wrote in her diary that Miryam's father was an Indian doctor of Portuguese ancestry. But, a year or so ago, Miryam discovered that what her mother had written could not be true because of a DNA test that she had done to confirm a diagnosis that she suffered from a genetic disease inherited from the father's side.

"An illness my mother suffered from," Rodrigues added after a short pause with some emphasis, leaving the sentence to hang in the air.

"Then Miryam *is* your daughter," Esperanza said in a tone that sounded like a question and raised her eyebrows.

"The DNA analysis that I did after Miryam told me about her diagnosis confirms it."

"Had you already suspected it, professor?" Paola asked.

"I suspected it from the moment we met, although that was not the case for Miryam. Perhaps what Monica told her about her father made her blind of the resemblance. She doesn't think that now, of course. Now she says that the resemblance is amazing."

"Wow. It must have been a big surprise for you," Esperanza said and covered her mouth with both hands.

"Now I understand why that first encounter must have been shocking," Paola added.

"Hmm," Rodrigues muttered. "When we met, that is, when we first spoke to each other, the experience was more like *recognizing* her than meeting for the first time. She looks like Monica when it comes to the color of her skin and her hair and her eyes, and the shape of her face, but beyond that she looks like me, in a very surprising way. We have the same nose and mouth, and when we are side by side, it seems that we have the same type of body; we are both slender and broad shouldered."

"Do you get along with her?" Paola asked.

"We have similar temperaments. We are both very independent, and also introverted and a little melancholic. We've become good friends, actually. We have even worked together on some projects. She is a lawyer who specializes in international law. She's come to Tokyo several times in the last two years"

"To Tokyo?" Paola asked and looked Rodrigues in the eye.

"Sorry, I meant that she has gone to Tokyo several times. I'm not completely used to being here, as you can see."

"Did you live in Tokyo?"

"Twenty-five years, and maybe a few more. I don't know if I'll ever get used to living anywhere else."

"I lived in Tokyo for a while, professor," Paola said and felt a knot in her stomach.

"Really? When?"

"A short stay, only for six months about a year ago, give or take," Paola replied and looked sideways at Esperanza who seemed taken aback.

"Did you work there?"

"Well, yes," Paola hesitated. "At a Colombian trading company," she said, instantly regretted it. For some reason she thought that Rodrigues was the kind of person who could tell right away when someone was lying. "Yes, professor, I learned a lot in Japan," Paola went on. "The business arena is very competitive, and people are very disciplined. You have to be very committed with what you do. Like they say, *Gambatte*, work hard!"

"Yes, people work hard, sometimes unnecessarily so," Rodrigues said and feigned a smile. Perhaps he had something else to say, but he preferred not to. "My apologies for changing the subject," he added in a firmer tone. "I went too long on the tangent of my biological daughter. Since I saw the photos of the bargueño, I have not stopped thinking about the issue of inheritance, I mean of lineage. Some of the descendants of the Bogotá family I told you about earlier decided to get DNA tests to find out if they had a

Jewish origin. I don't know if you're aware, but DNA testing has become very popular in Europe and the United States, and here too, as my students have told me. Either way, the results of the tests confirmed that they had Jewish ancestry. The family didn't make the results public. Apparently the DNA tests are an apple of discord for the family. However, one of them, the youngest if I'm not mistaken, who now lives in New York and is a writer, did a video that he posted on YouTube where he talks about this. It's a long story full of drama, but to make it short, this young man has approximately ten percent Ashkenazi Jewish blood, and according to him, his mother has twice that percentage, which would give credibility to the Jewish lineage hypothesis. Though it doesn't tell us how many generations ago, and whether these ancestors were aware of that lineage and not to mention where they came from, Ashkenazi bloodlines are from Eastern Europe, not from the Iberian Peninsula where the majority of mestizo Colombians trace their ancestry, and where the Jews were mostly Sephardic."

"Sephardic?" Esperanza asked.

"From Sefarad, the Hebrew name for Spain," confirmed Rodrigues who had changed his tone of voice during his monologue to a neutral one without the Bogotá affectation. "There are others, the Mizrahi, who are descendants of the Jewish communities of the Middle East and Africa," he added.

"We didn't know," Paola clarified and looked sideways at Esperanza, who seemed genuinely interested in what Rodrigues was saying, though it could also be part of her strategy to seduce him.

"Yes of course, excuse me taking so much time with these details. Sometimes I go off on a tangent for too long," said Rodrigues, sipping his lemonade. "In any case," Rodrigues went on, "I bring all this up because it occurred to me that a DNA test might be relevant in this case. Although I am aware that it may not be necessary."

"What do you mean relevant?" Esperanza asked and made a grimace of not understanding.

"A DNA analysis could establish that you are related to that family," Rodrigues replied. "Which would partially explain why your grandfather had the *Arca de Noé*. The idea came to my mind because of something Paola said. Although perhaps you said it by mistake, a *lapsus linguae*, a slip of the tongue."

Paola and Esperanza looked at each other.

"When you told me about your grandfather's inheritance," Rodrigues went on, "you said that he had put the bargueños in the San Benito room where you stored unused or old stuff at home. At first, I didn't think it odd that you said San Benito's room and not San Alejo's room, which is the proper term in Spanish for that sort of storage room. But later, when I was telling you about the expulsion of the Jews from Spain and the Inquisition, I suddenly remembered that a San Benito or *Sanbenito* was a garment, a cap that penitents and heretics had to use by order of the Inquisition."

"And the Jews were heretics," Paola said.

"Yes, that's why I thought maybe your grandfather could be of Jewish origin, perhaps without knowing it. Among the Spanish Catholics who arrived with the conquest and in the colonial era, there were some who were converts. And among those converts, there were some who still kept some of their Jewish traditions, secretly, of course. I imagine that over time some of them found it difficult to continue with those traditions, especially when marrying couples of another ethnic origin and religion, and the only traditions they could keep were odds and ends, some words or phrases, for example."

"Like calling San Benito a San Alejo's room?" Paola asked and looked at Esperanza, who also seemed surprised with what Rodrigues was saying.

"Truth be told, word usage is a weak clue," Rodrigues replied. "But sometimes those weak clues make up the thread that binds us to the fabric of the past. Up until now, you haven't told me anything about it, so I assume you don't know anything about a Jewish ancestor in your family, right?"

"No, God forbid," Esperanza burst out, perhaps by reflex because she immediately covered her mouth as if she had regretted saying it. "I mean, no," she added, her face slightly flushed.

"My parents are very Catholic," Paola added. "And as far as I know, my grandparents too; all except my grandfather Rafael, who used to say he was an agnostic, something that made my dad laugh, but annoyed my mom to no end."

"Well, being Jewish is not just about religion. It's also a matter of lineage; and of genetics, of course," Rodrigues said. "What do you know about him?"

"My dad used to tell us stories about him, but my mom said that they were mostly made up or blown out of proportion," Paola replied. "According to dad, when my grandfather was young, he was a carpenter and a cabinetmaker and made the bargueños, a trade he said he learned from his father, who in turn learned from his father, that is from my great-great-grandfather. He sold those pieces of furniture to very well-off people in Bogotá. But it seems that he was also a kind of healer and knew many medicinal plants and helped people, which was what took him away from the family. According to my mom, one day when I was eight or nine years old, my grandfather left town and abandoned my grandmother. He said that his destiny was to look for people who needed the healing potions he made. After several years, five or six, he came back; it seems that someone told him that my grandmother was very sick, and he came to see if he could heal her. But the poor thing had a very advanced cancer and died almost at the same time of his return. He was very sorry for leaving her alone. My father, who at first was very angry with him, told him that he forgave him, and that it would be best if he stayed with us, that he was too old to continue with his journeys. That's how he came to live with us. The only thing he brought home was a suitcase with some clothes, and a large trunk where he had three or four bargueños which he kept in that room under the stairs that *he* called San Benito's room."

"So, your parents didn't refer to it that way?"

"Maybe yes, but I don't remember, professor," Paola said. "I'd have to ask them."

"At home we didn't have a San Alejo or San Benito room," Esperanza said, a look of concern on her face. Paola thought that she was trying hard to remember anything her grandfather ever said. He was very fond of her. Whenever they had a family reunion, her grandfather always said, in jest, that Esperanza—which in Spanish translates as 'hope'—was the family's hope, and he invariably would burst out laughing.

"A complicated inheritance," Paola said. In her mind appeared the image of her grandfather with the whole family, on her quinceañera, her fifteenth birthday, and her most frequent memory.

Esperanza, her brow slightly wrinkled, nodded with her head and looked sideways at her mobile. Perhaps it was time to leave for the meeting they had that evening.

"I would say intriguing," Rodrigues added and looked towards the sandstorm that was still whistling through the sliding door that led to the balcony and to the hidden sea beyond.

NINE

Tony was checking Sonatine's accounts on the office computer when someone knocked on the door. He was in a bad mood that afternoon. The calculations he was working on did not add up, or better said, they did not reveal the money laundering schemes he knew they contained. He had been working on this task for three days, but so far, he had not found any clues. After a few moments, there was another knock, and very much in spite of himself, he got up from his chair and opened the door.

"Sorry to bother you," It was Wendy's friend, Fardan, who he met at the jazz festival the week before. "Maybe I should have called earlier to make an appointment."

Tony told him not to worry, and to come in and take a seat. He asked him what he could do for him. Despite his obfuscation, he thought it was providential that Fardan came to his office today. Last night, he had called Vladimir and had discussed the possibility of buying one or two apartments in partnership in the building where Wendy lived, which was owned by Fardan's family real estate company.

"Wendy gave me your phone number," Fardan said as he took a seat. "But I thought it would be better if we spoke in person," he added and placed the two mobiles that he was carrying in his hand into the lap of his white *dishdasha*.

"I get it. I don't like talking on the phone either, unless there's no other way," Tony said. "Can I offer you a coffee or tea?"

"No thanks, I just had a coffee," Fardan replied, a nervous smile on his face as if he was about to give bad news or ask him to do something that he would rather not do himself.

"I'm all ears."

"It is business matter, a translation in fact, and some consulting on cultural matters."

Tony felt a knot in his stomach. "Does it concern Japanese investors?" he asked.

"Not at the moment," Fardan replied and gave a hearty laugh. "It's a bit complicated," he went on. "My father, whose name is also Fardan, Fardan Al Fardan, is a collector of works of art and antiquities, especially from Al Andalus—Andalusia, as you say—and he's interested in obtaining, I mean in purchasing, a work of art currently in Colombia."

"In Colombia?" Tony asked somewhat surprised. He had not thought about Colombia in a long time. The word itself, *Colombia*, sounded foreign to him. Although, at that moment it filled him with relief that it was not something related to Japan, the bittersweet scenario of his past to which for the time being he was forbidden to return.

"Yes, in Bogotá," Fardan went on. "He has already expressed his interest in acquiring the work. It is an object for which he is willing to pay whatever the price—within reason—but there seems to be another interested party, an art historian who works at a university in Madrid, and we need to know whether this party is likely to outbid my father should there be a bidding war. Unfortunately, all the information on the Internet about this person is in Spanish…"

"That would be the translation," Tony said.

"Yes, and there are also other legal documents, authentication certificates, if I'm not mistaken. All this would be confidential, otherwise we would have called a translation company," Fardan added, looking sideways at his watch. It was close to sunset, and soon there would be a call to prayer from the mosque around the corner.

"And the consulting?"

"That would come later, but it would be about helping my father to acquire this work of art. There is no need to go to Colombia. My father prefers to keep a low profile. Everything will be done by videoconference, except for the purchase itself. One of my father's lawyers would do that.

"I would gladly do the translations," Tony said. "As for helping with the purchase of the work, I'm not sure I can be of much help, I don't know much about art…"

"Sorry to interrupt you, Tony," Fardan said in haste. "My father is well advised in matters related to art. He works with a Moroccan art critic and curator based in Seville, who is already in Colombia, and has had the opportunity to see and examine the work and to certify its authenticity. The consulting we are talking about is on negotiation styles, business etiquette, to put it broadly. My father is aware that cultural differences can lead to misunderstandings.

"Well, in that case, you can count on me."

***

That night, Tony went to Wendy's apartment for dinner. He had not seen her since the first night they spent together. Wendy had gone to Kuwait to attend a conference and had just returned the night before. They talked on the phone several times, and during each call, Tony had felt an intense desire for her. Unlike him, Wendy was very skilled in the art of virtual seduction; she was able to turn an ordinary conversation into an erotic game with a velvety tone of voice tinged with irony, which subjugated Tony and left him wanting for more.

"I feel like I've known you for a long time," Wendy said in greeting.

"Maybe we knew each other from before," Tony replied. "The other night when you told me that you went with your students to a Latino club in Roppongi and you knew the manager, I realized that it could be a Venezuelan friend of mine."

"Yes, of course, César is Venezuelan. For some reason I thought he was Mexican," Wendy said and gave herself a light pat on the cheek.

"Did you ever go during the week? I could only ever go either on a Monday or Tuesday. I was often busy on the weekends."

"Yes, of course, I always went on a weeknight. It was impossible to get a table on the weekends, unless you joined the dance classes."

"See, maybe it was there that we met."

"A good reason to celebrate that we met again," Wendy said in the velvety tone she used on the phone and gave him a bottle of wine for him to open and pour them drinks.

Tony nodded, and felt that he had given up control of what happened between them once and for all. That night Wendy wore a light blue Arab *jalabiya* dress that went down to her feet and had her hair pulled back in a ponytail.

They toasted in silence and watched the outline of

the city in the distance. The sky was clear, and a waning moon peered out of a bank of clouds over the creek towards the sea.

***

After dinner and back in the living room with a glass of wine in hand, Tony told Wendy that he was going to tell her something of his past that she should know now rather than later.

Wendy arched her eyebrows and smiled.

"My job in Tokyo was to manage a hostess bar with exotic dancers," Tony went on. "The girls were mostly from Eastern Europe, though there were also some Latinas, Brazilians, and Colombians. It was not an illegal job. I had my documents in order, but my bosses were, well, they are still, *yakuza* mobsters. I came to Dubai to get away from them. It's a complicated mess, but it's not serious, a misunderstanding really. It will sort itself out in a few months, perhaps even sooner."

"Are they looking for you?"

"At first, yes, but not anymore. They've banned me from going back to work, though, so I'll have to stay in Dubai for a while. At least until the work visa that my business partner in Tokyo helped me to get expires."

"I imagined something like that," said Wendy, and she smiled at him half-heartedly. "I mean, I figured you were in Dubai running away from something. I think a good percentage of expats in this city are running away from something. Someone should write a book, a novel, about this or even make a movie. Either way, don't worry about it. I'm not in the habit of judging people for their past. I'm glad you told me now, though."

Tony nodded and looked at Wendy out of the corner of his eye. Wendy did not seem bothered by what he told her. If anything, she looked relaxed, as if his revelations had the effect of putting her at ease.

For a moment, they both looked at one of the skyscrapers on the other side of the creek that had a light show projected on all its sides. It made it look as if it were rotating on its own axis.

"I worked in one of those clubs," Wendy said suddenly, her gaze still in the distance. "As a hostess, I wasn't a dancer. I wouldn't have done it," she added. "I wouldn't have been good at it; I wouldn't have known how. I was going through a rough patch back then. My father had just died, and I was in Tokyo doing my research for my master's degree. I worked as an English teacher in the evenings, but a friend told me that as hostess I could earn more than double per hour, so I went to the first hostess club I found in Ginza, near where I lived at that time, and they hired me right away. It was a good place, I mean it was expensive and exclusive, though from time to time some *yakuza* came who had some business with the club owner. The Japanese girls took care of them. I never sat with them. I didn't last long at that job, three or four weeks. Not because I resented playing the role of a submissive woman who serves men their drinks, lights their cigarettes, is amazed with their tales, and laughs at their jokes, whether good or in bad taste. For me, it was the opposite. They were the ones who entertained me with their nonsense and clumsiness, and their pathetic attempts at seduction. I quit because I hated that it was always all the same, that all of them did and said the same things, that everything was so predictable and mundane. It put me in a bad mood. Sometimes, I would tell them things I later regretted, veiled insults, ironic comments that some of them understood though pretended they did not, or they took it as a joke, as if it were part of the entertainment."

Tony nodded his head to indicate he was paying attention and understood. He thought it wise not to make any comments or ask any questions. It was better to let Wendy tell him what she wanted, in her own way and in her own time. Despite himself, he thought of Adriana for whom hostess work was easy and fun. A blessing she once said, perhaps because she knew well the dark side of night life.

"I was also lucky that the *mamasan* at the bar was very kind to me," Wendy continued. "She acted as if I were in her care, like I was some sort of relative. I'm aware that not all girls have the same luck. I know there are some who do badly and end up on the street or working at a dive bar."

Tony nodded again, and thought of the streets of Kabukichō, Tokyo's red-light district, where he had met his friend and partner, Vladimir. Back then he managed a small bar in a back alley near a metro station where he ended up lost one night while looking for something he no longer remembered.

"I imagine you'd like to know how things work in Dubai," Wendy said and got up for an instant, then sat down again, facing him with her legs folded under. "Since we saw each other at the jazz festival, I knew we would be having this conversation."

"I'm glad we're on the same page," Tony said and moved so that he could face her and felt certain that they would be good together as business partners, should she be open to work with him.

"To begin with, there are no hostess bars or exotic dancer clubs as such in this country; the current labor laws would not allow it," Wendy said, her tone businesslike as if she was discussing a marketing strategy. "What we have are several types of bars, clubs, and massage parlors where men—and perhaps women too, I haven't heard about any such place, just rumors, though it wouldn't surprise me—go looking for a sex partner for a few hours or for the whole night. I know of it because people tell me about it, and because it's very visible in some areas like your neighborhood, my old neighborhood."

"Who controls that?"

"I don't know," Wendy replied. "The police, I suppose. Everybody knows about them, but nobody cares enough to make them disappear."

"What interests me is what you do…"

"I figured," Wendy said and returned her gaze to the creek. A luxury yacht with all its lights on was berthing on a pier at the hotel across from them. "What I do is manage models and hostesses," she went on after a short pause. "I pay them an hourly wage that is comparable to what they would get at a modeling agency. If they want to date or do whatever with one of the clients, they have to do it on their own time. I don't get involved, and I don't care. Most of the women I work with have a full-time gig with a modeling agency. It's overtime work for them, for me too."

"Don't you have to report that?"

"It isn't necessary," Wendy replied." I mean, there is no one to report it to. Remember that we don't pay income taxes in this country. I am also a friend of the agency's manager, and she makes sure everything is in order. She is Colombian, you know."

"Colombian?"

"Yes, she's the one Fardan junior is in love with. Your parents are from Colombia, right? Do you have citizenship there?"

"Yes, but haven't been there in many years."

"I would like to go sometime. I've heard good things about it."

"Like what?"

"That it is a very diverse country and very dynamic. I like Garcia-Márquez's magical realism, and Caribbean music, salsa…"

"Ah, tropical Colombia."

"You say it in an ironic tone."

"Truth be told, it's a love-hate relationship."

"In what sense?"

"Don't mind me. It's something personal, a family matter. I love them all, but I appreciate the distance that separates us."

"Don't you get along?"

"I didn't get along with my father," Tony replied. "He is a very difficult man. Nothing pleases him, and he lives in a permanent bad mood. I don't really talk to him. We have never been able to talk; we don't have anything to tell each other, and we have nothing in common."

"And your mother?"

"She is very affectionate, but I can't talk with her either. I don't understand her. She is very submissive, always doing what my father says even if it is crazy. They have always lived on a tight budget. I mean, they don't have much money, they live paycheck to paycheck, and yet they worry about appearances. They live in a fancy neighborhood, well above their income. My father works as a public notary, and what he earns is barely enough for the rent and to pay their expenses. I send them money every month, my older sister too."

"And how do you get along with your big sister?"

"We get along, but she is ten years older than me. She lives in New York and works in a hospital; she is a nurse."

"Did you live with her in New York?"

"Yes, for a while. She helped me a lot, she was the one who helped me to get out of Colombia. Thanks to her, I became a legal resident in the United States. She also helped me when I was learning Japanese."

"Oh yes, you told me that you were a translator. How was that? I confess that when you told me it seemed strange to me."

"That I was a translator?"

"That you were a Japanese translator in New York."

"Yes, I suppose it is not *usual* for a Colombian or a Latino to be a Japanese translator in New York."

"How sensitive you are," Wendy said and smiled.

"I'm messing with you. From very early on I had a taste for everything Japanese. Do you remember that when you asked me yesterday about my favorite movies, I told you the Noriko trilogy by Yazujirō Ozu? It may seem strange, but from the first time I watched them at an art cinema in Bogotá, I identified with the characters and the world of the films. Don't laugh but they made me—and they still make me—feel nostalgic. A nostalgia for a country and a culture that are not mine. And the fifties!"

"Did you learn Japanese watching movies?"

"Movies helped a lot, but I did study Japanese language and culture at Hunter College. It was not easy to become a translator, though. It's a long story, to tell you the truth..."

"The night is young," Wendy said.

"Okay. I'll tell you a little more tonight, but I must warn you that there are several surprises."

"I love surprises."

"We'll see," Tony said and drank the wine left in his glass. Wendy made as if she was going to serve him another, but Tony shook his head and smiled, he wanted to pace his drinking that evening.

"When I was in my last year of college, I met a Japanese woman, and I married her."

"I didn't know you were married," Wendy said and knitted her brow.

"I'm not now. It was a marriage of exoticisms."

"I've never heard such a thing."

"We were each fascinated by the culture of the other. I mean that we each fell in love with an idea, not with an actual person."

"Oh, I know what you're talking about."

"She worked in a Japanese bookstore near Rockefeller Center in Manhattan where I went on weekends to find books that would help me with my studies. They had a billboard where people posted ads, and I put one which proposed an exchange of Spanish classes for Japanese classes. The same day I put it in, she called me, and we agreed to meet twice a week to practice each other's language, one day me, the other her. Unfortunately, her level of Spanish was very low, and we decided that instead of teaching her Spanish, I would teach her how to dance salsa."

"Did it work?"

"Yes, it worked great. My Japanese improved, and she learned to dance well, better than me, in fact."

"And that's how the romance came about?"

"We got married after three months."

"Why did you divorce?"

"The problems started as I got better at Japanese. At some point my Japanese was better than her English, and we switched completely to Japanese. It was then that I realized that she was another person in Japanese, different from the one I had fallen in love with. She didn't know herself well; she was very insecure, and she needed someone to help her unravel the mess she had in her head. She wanted to be free, or freer, or less conventional, but something stopped her and prevented her from being who she wanted."

Wendy narrowed her eyes and took her chin in her hands. "It sounds sad," she said.

"I didn't know what to do. I suggested that we go to Japan. I thought that being there, surrounded by family and friends, she would feel better about herself."

"And that's how you went to Japan?"

"Yes, and I was right; she felt better. She re-established her relationship with her mother with whom she had had problems in the past. But then, *I* started having problems."

"You didn't feel right in Japan?"

"On the contrary, I felt good, but not in my marriage; I began to feel that the relationship was suffocating me, and that I needed to be free. Also, I didn't like my job as a language teacher. The school did not pay me well, and I had to travel a lot by train. Fortunately, she realized what was happening to me, and little by little, she let me go. Ironically, since we were divorced, we became good friends. She helped me change jobs. She introduced me to her half-brother who owned a Latin bar in Roppongi, and I started working there as a manager. The place was not very good; the clientele was a bit dodgy, to say the least. From time to time, we had to close it because the police would come and raid it looking for drugs and *chimpira*, low-level *yakuza*."

"Was your brother-in-law a mobster?"

"No, but he knew a few, and how things worked. He knew who was pulling the strings in the area."

"It's always good to know who's pulling the strings," Wendy echoed and left the phrase hang in the air.

"As you do," Tony added.

"As I do?"

"I see that you hid Fardan's father pictures."

"Sorry?"

"The other night I saw the photograph where you are with him in Tokyo."

"Oh! Wendy cried out and laughed. "You caught me. But I didn't marry him; far from it. It was a short-lived affair. It wouldn't have worked anyway. When you told me about your Japanese wife, I thought about him. When I met him in Tokyo, he was a different man. He behaved differently; he was shy, kind, sympathetic. But, with time, I understood that all this was a façade. When I came to the UAE, I realized what kind of man he was."

"What kind was that?"

Wendy tapped her chin before she answered. "Fardan is an authoritarian macho man," she went on. "He doesn't tolerate being contradicted even when he is wrong. If you listen to him talk about others, especially women, you will get an unpleasant surprise; he's a little medieval when it comes to gender issues. He's got a good heart, though, but I could never be with a man like that. Do you know how I met him? I was his English teacher, though he didn't need one. I think he enrolled as a student in the school I taught at just to talk and flirt with me and the other foreign teachers. I think he had lots of free time. He was in Japan doing business, something to do with heavy machinery. He dated Japanese women, too, though I think he didn't fare well with them. He was the one who helped me come to Dubai. A month or two after he left Tokyo. He sent me an email where he told me that there was a job at Dubai International University that would be perfect for me. It was to manage the foreign student exchange program—something I did in Australia when I was in college—and he copied the message to the director of Human Resources of the university. I had to send my credentials and do a video interview, but I think it was a mere formality; the job was already mine."

Tony looked at Wendy and realized that her wine glass was empty. He would serve them another round.

TEN

The first document that Tony translated was a photo-copy of a four-page will that was dated April tenth of nine-teen-forty-two in which the names of the witnesses were redacted, as were their signatures. The text itself was brief; after a few introductory sentences that indicated that the owner, a man named Nicolás Ruiz, was in good health, both physically and mentally, it said that he bequeathed the antiques listed below to Bogotá's Museo del Virreinato. The following paragraph listed ten articles, eight bargueños with marquetry and two medieval bestiaries, in Latin. The next page was a low-resolution copy of a document dated December first, eighteen hundred and thirty. It said that the bestiaries had belonged to the descendants of that great philosopher of their faith. There was another phrase after that, but it was it was blurred and illegible.

The following five-page document was a lawsuit against Nicolás Ruiz on behalf of his wife and two children. The text alleged that the testator suffered from dementia at the time it was done, and that therefore it should be annulled.

Attached to it, there was a medical certificate from a psychiatric hospital in Bogotá on behalf of the testator that stated that he was hospitalized and under the care of the institution throughout the month of April, nineteen-forty-two.

The third and last document of six pages was the decision of a local court in Bogotá, dated July fifteenth, nineteen-forty-three, that noted the annulment of the will dated April tenth of nineteen-forty-two.

The background check on the art historian was easier than he had anticipated. On the faculty website of the university in Madrid where she worked, he found a link to a bilingual English-Spanish personal page with a short biography and a list of her academic credentials, publications, and the papers she had given in conferences around the world. The only thing that caught his attention from the list was a paper she published recently on medicine in medieval Andalusia. Perhaps he would read it later as it was on an open access online journal. From the biography, he learned that she was forty-five years old, single, and that her favorite pastime was reading historical novels. Because of her academic credentials—an undergraduate degree from a well-known Jesuit university in Bogotá and an MA and PhD from Columbia University in New York—he speculated that she came from a middle- or upper-class background. From what he read in internet forums, the salaries for scholars of her rank in Spain were not very high. Even if her family in Colombia were really wealthy, he doubted that she could compete in an auction with Fardan's family, which from what he had read in a business magazine published in Dubai had one of the greatest fortunes in the Middle East, perhaps in the world.

***

That afternoon, Tony called Fardan and gave him a summary of his findings.

"Great," Fardan said. "Now we need to get a good law firm in Bogotá to help us acquire the art works I mentioned. Do you know any? The UAE Embassy in Bogota gave us a list, but my father would prefer to have more options. It has to be a firm that could work with the one in London that handles most of his legal affairs."

Tony told him that he wasn't sure he could help with that, but that he would try. After he hung up, he wrote to an old high school friend who worked for a large law firm in San Francisco. Though, he wasn't sure if he was a lawyer. The last time he heard from him, about a year or so ago, he was still in law school. If things worked out, he wouldn't tell Fardan or his father of his friendship. He preferred to keep an ace up his sleeve.

ELEVEN

Paola was about to step out with Esperanza to do some shopping when her mobile rang. "Sweetheart, I'm glad I found you," her mother said in her anguish-laden tone of delivering bad news. For an instant, Paola thought it was about her father who suffered from a heart murmur, but her mother went on without a pause. "We came across an obstacle in the matter of the bargueños. The curators are saying that the big bargueño belongs to the museum; that they can't figure out how your grandfather came to have it, and that they have to do an investigation! They say that the family that gave the bargueño to the museum has all the necessary documentation, and that they are going to put a legal restraint to prevent the bargueño from being sold or leaving the country!"

After this last outburst her mother finally paused, and in a more measured tone said that her Cousin Carmen knew a lawyer whom they were going to call that same afternoon.

"What do you think, sweetie?"

Paola was at a loss for words. What her mother told her

felt like a sentence imposed by a judge. After a moment, she sighed and told her not to worry, that everything was going to be all right, and that they should call the lawyer, but they should not commit to anything, least of all make a payment, and that she, in turn, would talk to a friend who was also a lawyer.

"Okay, baby, whatever you say," her mother said, her voice still full of anguish. "But what is this mess?" she asked suddenly, her tone now tinged with anger. Paola told her to calm down and summed up the conversation with Professor Rodrigues.

"Do you know if Grandfather Rafael had Jewish blood?"

"No, baby, nothing of the sort," her mother cried out. "How could you say that! Holy Mother of Jesus! Your grandfather had strange habits. He didn't touch pork as he said it was a forbidden delicacy, and he mocked priests and the Holy Father, but he never said anything about being a Jew. Your dad would've known; the old man was reserved with me, but not with your father, his son. He told him everything, absolutely everything, even things that your father was ashamed to hear. If your grandfather told him something about Jewish blood, he would've told me right away. You know how gossipy he is.

"But what does Jewish blood have to do with anything?"

"I already told you, mom," Paola replied and put her free hand on her head. Her mother was upset, and it was best not to go into any details. "Please tell Dad to call me as soon as possible."

"No need, baby," her mother replied. "He is here, stuck on the other side of the phone."

"God bless you, honey," her father said in the sweet tone he often used with her, though she noticed a little tremor in his voice. Perhaps he was also upset. "Your Grandfather

Rafael had many secrets," he went on. "But he never told me about being Jewish or having Jewish blood. We were very old-fashioned at home. We didn't talk about religion; I mean any other than the Catholic one. My father was not religious, you already know that, but he had his own ideas. He used to say that he was a theosophist, and that all religions were the same. Your grandmother, may she rest in peace, was very intolerant. She would tell your grandfather that he was the devil, and scolded him for saying such things in front of the children, and she would burst into tears."

Her father was about to say something else, but then he paused. Paola could not hear anything, perhaps her mother was telling him something, and he had covered the phone. "Sorry, sweetheart," her father said after a few seconds. "Your mom says what she always says; that the old man was crazy. But I don't think so. On the contrary, my father was intelligent and forthright as I've always told you. He did have strange ideas, but perhaps they were strange back then—not now. It seems to me that people are not so attached to religion nowadays. The other thing with him was that he said things that were hard to believe, and if he saw that you were hesitant, he would turn it into a joke so that you couldn't figure out whether it was true or not. So it was with the bargueños that we had at home when I was a child—there were several, not just the three that he brought home. I remember he once said that he made some of them, and that my grandfather—your great-grandfather—made the others. That time, he also told me that my grandfather was a prince who had come from a distant land where the wise men were from, and then burst out laughing. The old man had fun with me, though I was very serious and really wanted to know.

"One day when I was thirteen or fourteen years old,

he told me that if I decided to learn the trade, he would tell me everything I wanted to know. I said yes, I wanted to learn, and he was very happy. He told me that the first thing I had to do was to carefully read a little book that he kept with great zeal in his desk that would help me find *the good path, the way*. I hardly knew how to read back then; I didn't go to school much because my mother needed me at home to do some chores. The poor thing couldn't cope with everything she had to do. She was a seamstress, you know; she made caps to sell on the street to help with household expenses. What your grandfather earned selling his frames and bargueños and the potions of herbs to cure arthritis and rheumatism were not enough. There were seven of us at home, and my older sisters were already in high school and they did nothing but study! Anyway, I started reading the little book. I was very excited that I was going to learn my father and grandfather's trade, and that I was going to have many important clients like the ones my father had, though I was going to be more cunning with my money, which was what my mother said my father didn't have—she always said that the only thing he knew about money was how to spend it. But fate didn't allow it, you know what happened next..."

"Yes, Dad, I know," Paola said. "Grandad said from one day to the next that he was going on a trip, that he was going south to look for some herbs to make some ointments that were going to be the definitive cure for rheumatism, and he didn't return for five years. But what I wanted to ask you is if you know anything else about your grandfather, my great-grandfather, maybe the Jewish ancestry is on that side."

"What can I say about my grandfather," her father mumbled meditatively and once again there was a silence, perhaps another intervention or comment from her mother, who was surely still listening to the conversation with her ear stuck to the back of the phone. "Your mother says that on that side there can be no Jewishness," he went on, a trace of annoyance in his voice. "She is convinced that side of the family was more Papist than the pope, and perhaps she is right about that, though she barely knew them; I knew them a little more, of course, but not much more. We had little to do with them because my grandmother died giving birth to a girl, who would have been my dad's younger sister, my aunt, and my grandfather soon remarried to a woman from a prominent and very well-off family. I don't really remember him. He died when I was twelve or thirteen; he apparently suffered from a rare disease that affected his heart. My father used to say that he was a very wise man who knew a lot about botany and about the herbal remedies of the Indians who lived where he was from, and that he taught him all that too."

When her father said that, Paola remembered that Grandfather Rafael had told her about a large farm where he lived as a child and learned the secrets of medicinal plants. He told her that when she went to medical school, he was going to teach her those secrets to complement her education. The poor sweet old man loved her a lot. When she could not get into medical school, he told her not to worry, and to major in something else that would benefit others, and that he was going to teach her what he promised anyway. Paola closed her eyes, and in her mind, she saw her grandfather's face. *Poor sweet old man*, she thought. It was a good thing he never heard of all the bad things that happened to her in Tokyo; it would have broken his heart.

"That's all I remember about your great-grandfather darling," her father said.

Paola asked him if her great-grandfather had more children.

"There were four more," he replied. "I never met them. they lived in Bogotá. His second wife was very uppity; I told you she was from a very wealthy, upper class family. She barely allowed my grandfather to visit my father to teach him how to make the frames and bargueños, which is all he left to him—to you—because in the end your inheritance is the bargueños that your grandfather and great grandfather made."

"And that lady, the one who married my great-grandfather, was her surname Valenzuela?" Paola interrupted.

"Yes, of course. How did you know?"

"I'll tell you later, Daddy," Paola said and felt suddenly euphoric. She thought that Professor Rodrigues had a good instinct and perhaps all of it was just a family affair. "Please ask Cousin Carmen for the lawyer's email address. I'll write to him myself; I think it's better that way."

TWELVE

Esteban told Paola that of course they could meet in the afternoon at the mall around the corner from his office in Bur Dubai, and that he would send the address by SMS.

Esperanza had offered to could go with her because she had a business appointment with some Emirati clients that she could not postpone. She looked a little upset. She did not like the idea of discussing the matter of the bargueño with Esteban. She argued that she liked Professor Rodrigues' idea of consulting with a lawyer specializing in art law better.

"Esteban doesn't know about those things, and to tell you the truth, I wouldn't trust him or his friends," she added.

"Don't worry, cousin. I know what I'm doing," Paola replied. "If what Esteban tells me doesn't sound right, I'll call the professor again. But just to ask him to send me the name of the lawyer he knows. What happens with the professor is that he wants to get fully involved to thoroughly investigate the history of the bargueño, and that seems unnecessary to me, even dangerous. I think he would be of more help to the museum in Bogotá than to us who need the money right now. When he told me that his Dutch colleague was investigating something similar about a Portuguese Jew of the Middle Ages who also wore a turban, I decided that was as far as I would deal with him. I don't care who the old man in the turban is. What I want to know is how much we can sell the bargueños for!"

"As you wish, cousin," Esperanza said. "If Esteban Garrido Esquire tricks you or swindles you, don't tell me I didn't warn you."

Paola took the metro to go to see Esteban. It was the first time she used public transportation. Indeed, it was the first time that she went alone to a part of the city that was not in her neighborhood. Before she left, Esperanza told her to take an Uber back and forth, but she decided that it was time to do things her way.

The metro was full, but Paola found one empty seat next to an Arab woman wearing an *abaya* and a head scarf at the end of the car reserved for women and children. From what she could see from the next car, most of the passengers in the metro were men, some from South Asia, Indian and Pakistani, others from Arab countries and the Philippines. She felt uncomfortable and out of place, as if her presence there was unusual or strange. The Arab woman next to her threw her angry glances, perhaps disapproving of the tight dress she was wearing, though it allowed no cleavage and fell below the knees. Two Pakistani men in *salwar kameez,* who were standing at the edge of the neighboring car, would not stop looking at her. Their gaze, however, somewhat indifferent and distant, as if contemplating something new and indecipherable.

Oddly, one of the Pakistani men reminded her of her grandfather, who was also tall with angular features, a dark complexion and gray eyes that sometimes looked green. She closed her eyes and, in her mind, saw a photograph of him when he was about twenty or thirty years old that she left behind in her apartment in Tokyo in her haste to escape the *yakuza*. An Israeli friend, a dancer who worked in the same club, had told her that her grandfather resembled her uncle, who lived in Tel Aviv, and she had laughed at her comment, though she understood why since her friend looked like a little like her. Although now that she thought about it, she looked much more like Esperanza who had a thinner face and eyebrows that were closer together.

A few stops past a large park that marked the entrance to the old part of the city, the metro went underground which meant that her exit was next according to the metro map. When she was about to get off the car, she ran into an older man, perhaps Arab or Persian—she still could not distinguish one from the other—who wanted to enter the car without allowing her and the other passengers to exit. She let him pass, and as she did, the old man's face reminded him of her grandfather once again. What madness it was, she thought, that in less than an hour she would find her grandfather's face in men of so many diverse nationalities.

***

Esteban was texting on his mobile when she arrived. He shook her hand and said he was glad to see her, something that took her by surprise; it sounded like a compliment.

After they ordered cappuccinos, Paola thanked him for coming, and told him about her inheritance and the bargueño and what the curators of the museum reported.

"It sounds like a property issue that could easily be resolved," Esteban said and crossed his arms. He was wearing a formal suit with a tie, which gave him an executive look,

108

very different from what Paola remembered from the first time they met. "What you said about the documentary evidence that the family is supposed to have sounds like a museum strategy to make time," he added. "We would need to see what kind of documents they're talking about, of course. It could be a will and testaments and property titles, and things of that nature. That the piece might be a twin of the one in the museum certainly helps. The question at the core of this case is why your grandfather had it in his possession."

"Let's say it's a family matter," Paola replied. "It's a bit complicated because it is a matter of lineage. I might tell you more later, but for now, it's all I can tell you."

Esteban looked Paola in the eye and gave a slight growl, as if he was meditating on something.

"I could recommend a law firm in Bogotá that I work with," he said. "They are very efficient and often hire detectives to thoroughly investigate cases. Something tells me that you may find those services useful."

"Are they property lawyers?"

"It's a firm that does all kinds of law."

Paola kept silent for a moment. Her instincts told her that Esteban could help her, that she could trust him, but that she had to keep him at a distance. She could not make the same mistakes she made with Tony and leave everything in his hands. She looked out the window facing the street, and something caught her attention. There was a commotion on the other side of the street, a fender bender between an SUV and a taxi. The two drivers were arguing next to their vehicles and paid no heed to the cars around them.

"The taxi driver is not going to fare well," Esteban said.

"Taxi drivers always get the short end of the stick," she interjected. She thought of her father, whose latest accident driving a taxi had prompted the current crisis her parents were facing.

"If the accident is his fault, and it's not the first time, he could lose his job and then be deported," Esteban added.

"It could be that bad?"

"The law is very strict in this country, especially with foreigners. I could tell you stories."

"The law is usually for poor people, for the peasants, as they say, isn't it?"

"That's how it is," Esteban replied. "I haven't heard that expression in a long time" Esteban said and took a sip of his cappuccino. "I feel right at home with you."

Paola looked at him and drummed at the table with her fingers. She wondered where Esteban's family was from. His accent today was different, more Andean, like hers.

"To get back to the case," Esteban said and cleared his throat. "What worries me is that even if you manage to prove that the piece belongs to you, the museum could very well put a restraint on its commercial use. They could claim that it is part of the country's cultural heritage, or something of that sort," he added.

"So, we couldn't sell it?"

"It's a possibility," said Esteban. "Maybe that would be the worst-case scenario. We would have to see what the lawyers in Bogotá say."

"Is there something that could be done?"

"To prevent that?"

Paola nodded.

"Anything is possible," Esteban replied and arched his eyebrows. "How much do you think those works are worth?"

"I don't know yet, but let's say a hundred thousand dollars."

"It is a considerable amount, but perhaps not enough to justify a long court battle. There are other alternatives, of course."

"Like what, for example?"

"I can't tell you that. It depends on what the lawyers say."

"If they say there's no way…"

"If there's money on the table, there is always an alternative, though it could be expensive."

"Do you trust them?"

"Completely."

"And, I would have to trust you."

"I haven't given you a reason not to," Esteban said and smiled in a way that seemed to Paola like a promise.

"Sorry about the other night, Esteban."

"Don't worry. You fell asleep like a little angel."

"Esperanza told me you had to carry me to bed," she said, and she felt her face reddened.

"I did it with pleasure."

"I owe you a date," Paola said, and thought from that moment on, she would take the lead in what she was sure would be a delicious affair.

THIRTEEN

One afternoon Tony ran into Professor Deenik who was leaving at that moment from his building with his terrier, Charlie, in tow. He had been thinking about the translation he did for Fardan and his father. He was particularly intrigued by the medieval bestiaries listed in the testament and wondered of the connection to the purchase of a Spanish colonial piece of furniture by a wealthy Gulf Arab in Dubai.

"Another beautiful twilight," he told the professor in greeting.

"This winter we've had some nice ones. Though not as dramatic as in the Caribbean, don't you think?"

"I think that in the Caribbean they are more colorful and intense," Tony replied. It had been a while, at least two weeks, since he had seen the professor, and he was eager for a good chat. Wendy was once again out of town, this time in Abu Dhabi attending some work event, and he had not talked to anyone the whole day.

"When I was little in Curaçao," Deenik said in a meditative tone, "my sisters and I went up every day to our rooftop to enjoy the sunset with our parents; it was my favorite time of day. It gave me peace."

"Are you from Curaçao?"

"Born and raised," Deenik replied and looked at the last glow of the day among the skyscrapers in the distance. The heat of the late afternoon had abated and a light cool breeze that suddenly came from behind ran swiftly between them. "We moved to the motherland, to Rotterdam, the land of my ancestors, when I turned fifteen," he added. "Do you know the island?"

"I went on vacation many years ago. I liked it a lot. It was during carnival. I had a great time."

"Ah, the carnival, yes," Deenik said in an animated tone, and he started to tell him about its origins, which had to do with the history of slavery on the island. It sounded like a topic he knew much about. Perhaps it was his specialization as a historian. At some point, he spoke of his childhood in Willemstad and mentioned his nanny, a woman of African origin, who told him stories and legends about animals and beasts that amused him, though they sometimes scared him.

Tony waited until Deenik finished his childhood story and asked him whether he knew anything about medieval bestiaries.

"See how this is a related topic, my dear friend," the professor replied. "Everything is related, of course, needless to say. We historians always go off on tangents precisely because of that. Did you know that our friend Kircher, who wrote the manuscript on the tower of Babel which we talked about the other night, wrote something about it?"

"I'm afraid not, professor."

"Well, that great Jesuit published a manuscript about Noah's Ark where he talks about the spurious animal species that had no place in the ark because they went against nature, such as the griffin, a chimerical creature that always appears in bestiaries, and was made of an eagle and a lion. But bestiaries are older than Kircher's text," Deenik continued in a lower voice, as if it were in confidence. "We already find them in the Greek and Roman classics. Later, they became popular in the Middle Ages, from the twelfth century on. In general, they are works of the imagination and mix reality with fantasy," Deenik noted.

"Were they published in books?" Tony asked, and to his mind came an image of a coloring animal's book that his mother gave him one Christmas, a sweet and distant memory.

"At first, they were manuscripts, and then they were published in books. They are interesting works. Most of them have a moralistic vein to reinforce the principles of Christian education, although sometimes they are openly anti-Semitic. This is how one topic is related to the other; the animal stories my nana told me when I was little were all together a sort of bestiary of the culture of her forefathers, who came to the island as slaves and had to convert to Christianity…"

Deenik paused and rubbed his beard, as if he were meditating on something. "How about we have a coffee, and we continue with the topic? Coffee helps me tie loose ends," he added.

"If you'd like we could go to Sonatine," Tony suggested. "Vicky, the cashier, will love to see Charlie."

Deenik said it was an excellent idea and added that it would be a pleasure for Charlie because very few restaurants in Dubai allowed dogs in their premises.

They chose a table by the window from which they could see the empty lot where they had been talking. A small group of five or six Filipino nannies gathered there now, as it was often the case after sunset; they would linger there for another ten or fifteen minutes. It was part of the rhythm of the neighborhood that Tony observed from his office and his apartment across the street.

After they ordered their beverages, Deenik commented that it was a coincidence that they were talking about bestiaries because one of the professors in the Islamic Studies Department at the university had recently published an essay about a famous fourteenth century Muslim bestiary. "Unfortunately, it's in Arabic, a language I can barely speak. But we are talking about an emeritus professor with a distinguished career. Someone who publishes on various topics," he added with some emphasis.

"You're lucky to have such distinguished scholars in Dubai," Tony noted, though he suspected that Deenik's emphasis was loaded with irony.

"Yes, though I can't tell you to what extent," he said and arched his eyebrows. "Now that we talk about the university," he went on in a confidential tone, "I've noticed a recent interest on the part of the administration for historical issues. It seems that we have a very important patron who is very interested in the Middle Ages in Al-Andalus, what we now call Andalusia. My guess is that it's one of the local sheikhs. It's hard to know for sure. The university's decisions are not at all transparent, as it should be in a monarchy like this one, I suppose."

Tony hesitated to say and simply nodded. What Deenik had just told him was perhaps the link between the bestiaries and the colonial furniture.

"Topics related to the history of Al-Andalus can be very contentious," Deenik continued. "Now that the Spanish government has invited the descendants of Jews who were expelled from that country in the fifteenth and sixteenth centuries, some social organizations in Spain and North

Africa have expressed their disagreement; they argue that they should also invite the descendants of Muslims expelled a few decades later to return. There has been a lot of talk about this topic at the university. I stay out of such discussions, which can sometimes be very heated. Besides, some of my past writings touch on those topics, though, from a Jewish perspective; it is a subject that in some way concerns me as it's part of my family's history."

"Excuse me, professor, what do you mean?"

"I beg your pardon. Sometimes I don't make myself clear. My ancestors were Sephardic Jews who were expelled from Portugal to the Netherlands, to Holland, in the sixteenth century, and from there they moved to Curaçao at that time of the Dutch crown."

"So, you are Jewish?"

"No, the history of my family, like that of the island, is of mixing; from my maternal line, I have Sephardic ancestors, six or seven generations ago. Some of those ancestors migrated to South America, by the way. You told me that your family was originally from Colombia, right? So, you see, we could even be relatives. If you don't mind my saying so, you have a bit of a Sephardic air."

"It could be," Tony said, "although, I know very little about my family history, except that on the mother's side I have Syrian blood from a very long time ago. My Israeli friends in Tokyo were always telling me that they had friends and relatives who looked like me. In turn, and to make a joke of it, I would tell them that my roots were Palestinian."

"You could very well be," Deenik said with a smile, and then he looked at Charlie, who, lying on the floor, seemed to be taking a nap.

FOURTEEN

Paola received an email from the law firm Esteban recommended stating they were willing to represent her with an attachment detailing their fees. She opened the document and saw that it was a mixed payment system; five thousand dollars to start, and twenty percent of the sale amount.

"Over my dead body," she said out loud to herself. Esperanza was at the office. That afternoon she had to work on a last-minute project; an event with one of the sheikhs, something she couldn't afford to say no to.

Still seething, Paola called Esteban.

"Don't worry," he said. "You can make the first payment in installments. They'll understand. Regarding the percentage, I think it's just about right. I doubt you can find a good firm that would do it for less. Did you hear from the curators?

"Yes," she muttered, and despite herself let out a sigh. "This morning when I talked to my father, I found out that they haven't finished their report. It seems that they can't agree with the meaning of the engravings. To tell you the truth, I don't understand what one thing has to do with the other."

"What about the engravings," Esteban asked, and lit a cigarette—Paola heard the click of his lighter and first puff of smoke.

"I really don't know," Paola replied. "Dad was told that they would have to consult with other art historians in Colombia and Spain because it was not only the engraving in the middle of a man with a turban—I told you about it, remember?—but also the other engravings of animals."

"They don't know what kind of animals they are," Esteban asked, his tone loaded with scorn or sarcasm.

"Dad asked the same thing, and they said it was not so much that, but their meaning all together. Don't ask me what that means because I don't know. I'm going to call Professor Rodrigues, maybe he can explain it to me."

"Before you do that, I have something to tell you. It's a message from the law firm that I recommended, something they can't tell you in writing. We can talk freely; this phone is safe."

"I'm all ears."

"First, I have to explain something to you. These pieces of furniture don't have any commercial value because they are legally registered as the museum's property, and they are properly insured, which means the insurance company has pictures and detailed descriptions of each of the art works, including the ones from your inheritance since they are temporarily in their charge. One of the firm's attorneys, someone with experience in art litigation, told me that it is not possible to lift the legal restriction that prevent their sale, particularly on the largest piece with the animal engravings, until they're satisfied that they weren't stolen. Remember that it is a government museum, and we are talking about the cultural heritage of the country. He also said that even if they're satisfied that that one piece wasn't stolen, they may place yet another legal restriction on its sale until they've properly researched it. In that case, the process would take quite a while, years perhaps. We both agree that if you want to sell the piece and spare yourself the grief of dealing with the museum, you'll have to somehow arrange it so that they're returned to you."

"I don't understand. If they're somehow returned to me, I won't be able to sell them…Didn't you say they have no commercial value?"

"If they are returned to you, you would be able to sell them to someone who's not interested in their provenance. An art collector with a taste for unique and exotic pieces, for example."

"You're talking in riddles, Esteban. Didn't you say this line was secure?"

"Okay. Let me put it another way. You would have to *take* the pieces out of the museum and sell them to a client who doesn't mind buying art works that can't be commercialized."

"You're talking about stealing them," Paola said loudly, in spite of herself.

"We are talking about your inheritance…"

"Would it be an armed robbery? I couldn't live with myself if someone is killed or injured," Paola said, and shook her head in negative as if Esteban was right there, facing her.

"No way an armed robbery," Esteban said quietly. "That would be too risky. We are talking about the time-tested method of offering a bribe, a decent amount in U.S. dollars and in cash to avoid taxes," he added in a tone leaded with irony.

"To the director of the museum?"

"Whomever has access to the security systems. I doubt that any senior administrator would take such a risk. Someone whom we have to investigate a little, but it would probably be a mid-range administrator, or the security staff."

"And if that doesn't work?"

"I'm sure it would work. My contact says that the best way would be to use a fake; that is, to take the original, and leave a copy, another twin."

"That sounds complicated. How much would that cost? You already know that we don't have that kind of money. And besides, who would make the other twin?"

"We'll talk about this when we meet tonight. As an advance, all I can tell you is that the interested party would cover the expenses, or rather, deduct them from the sale price. It's one of the firm's clients so it would be relatively easy to make all the necessary arrangements. As to whom would make the pieces, it would be artisans in Mexico, which is where the firm's client lives. Think about it. We'll talk about it in more detail tonight. I'll pick you up at seven, Okay?"

No sooner than Paola hung up, she felt a wave of unease, or perhaps fear, creeping through her body. What Esteban just told her, what he proposed, could well be the key to solving her problems, yet it was something that was wrong, not to mention illegal, a crime. Not that she had never done something that was wrong and illegal. But all of it added was mild in comparison. Just violations of minor laws, petty crimes from her past that she wanted to put behind her for good. If she said yes, to go ahead, and things didn't work out, she could be indicted as the mastermind of a crime which would undoubtedly be punished by imprisonment! Esteban and the other lawyer would wash their hands and leave her alone to pay for it. That was the way of the world for poor people like her. On the other hand, it would be a crime with many mitigating factors; after all, it was about *her* inheritance and family heirlooms, something that by law belonged to her; not to mention the fact that she needed the money to protect herself and her family from *real bona fide* criminals. The judge would have to weigh that on before passing sentence. The mere thought of going to prison terrified her. It was something she could not even imagine. The worst was not just the horror of confinement, or the lack of freedom, but what would come after. The shame she would feel would be a permanent stain in her life. Not to mention the pain it would cause her family, especially her mother. She was her only daughter, the apple of her eye, as she often told her.

There has to be another way, she told herself and got up—she had not moved from the sofa since she hung up the phone—and went to the kitchen to make some herbal tea to sooth her nerves. While waiting for the water in the kettle to boil, she thought of her father who always told her she had to think things through all the way and be realistic about risks. *You have to be courageous and not be afraid of anything,* he used to tell her.

She sat down with her cup of tea in the small round table they had in the kitchen. Through the window, she could see the open ocean and the palm shaped island with luxury hotels and residences on it for the rich and powerful. She thought she had to have a cool head. She needed that money to pay off her debts in Japan and to help her dad buy a new taxi. Of course, her debt was unfair. It was a fine she was charged for letting a woman escape, another Colombian woman who was being exploited. How unfair the world was with women! Or was it only to Colombian women? Her European woman friends in Tokyo were always happy. They didn't look stressed out by anything. They took off their clothes on stage as if it was nothing, or as if it were a joke. They didn't owe money to anyone, unless they used drugs. They went to Japan on their own and nobody hassled them. Nobody told them that because of their passport they had to start from the bottom. Things were better in Dubai, though she didn't really know. She no longer had to work in the minor leagues, in the worse dives. She wanted to be far away from that. But whether she liked it or not, she had to pay off her debt, she had no choice. She accepted the conditions out of her own free will, or so it seemed at that moment…if she didn't pay the *yakuza*, they told her they would collect the money from her family back in Colombia! She still had time, three more months, though what she earned in Dubai would not be enough, even if she worked full-time for two years without holidays with Esperanza. She had already done the numbers. A loan was impossible; the bank had barely approved a credit card with a very low limit. Esperanza could not help her; she had many personal and business expenses. Tony would have helped her if she had stayed in Japan—if the two had stayed in Japan—if they had talked things over with a cool head. Where was Tony? Where was he hiding? Perhaps her contacts in Japan knew of his whereabouts. She would make some calls later on.

FIFTEEN

The dinner was at a posh Moroccan restaurant in *Madinat Jumeirah*, a Middle Eastern themed shopping arcade in a tourist district along the southern coastal road. The place—closed to the public that night—had terracotta colored walls, slender columns with rounded horseshoe arches, large copper lamps hung from the ceiling, and an Art Deco feel that reminded Tony of Rick's Café, the main scenario of *Casablanca*, one of his favorite films.

Each place setting on the large rectangular table had a card with the name of a guest on it. Tony's was at one of the narrow corners. Wendy's was diagonally across from his, though not at the corner. That place was for someone with an Arab name, who would perhaps arrive late. The other diners were already at the table. Fardan Junior, who greeted them at the door of the restaurant sat on Tony's left.

Tony felt a little overwhelmed; he did not like formal events, much less with people he did not know. Wendy had called him at the last minute when he was getting ready to go out to meet her at a Japanese restaurant to let him know about the change of plans. She told him that Fardan's father had called her that afternoon to invite her, and that he had made it a point that she brought along her translator friend to personally thank him for his work.

Fardan's father was sitting directly across his son on the other side of the table. Like his son, he wore a cream-colored *kandura* and *guthra*, and wore rounded glasses that gave him a scholarly look. Seated to his right was a bald middle-aged man who, judging from the suit and tie he wore, could be a senior executive, perhaps of one of the conglomerates of companies that he controlled.

After a few minutes, the general chatter of the guests faded and Fardan's father stood up and thanked everyone for accepting his invitation. "Dear friends," he went on. "Tonight we meet to celebrate the signing of a memorandum of understanding between our foundation for cross cultural understanding in Dubai and Seville with an art museum in the city of Bogotá, in Colombia, for the creation of an annex dedicated to the legacy of Al-Andalus in the Americas, a project that will help boost the rapprochement between the Arab world and Latin America. My dear friend, Dr. Ahmed Al Morsi, a well-known scholar in the Arab World, and Dr. Farid Chad, the Colombian consul in Dubai, will say a few words about the project."

Ahmed Al Morsi was a tall and stocky middle-aged man with brown skin and dark hair, who had been standing by the table chatting with the maître d. After clearing his throat, he took a few steps forward and said a few words in Arabic, perhaps a compliment to Fardan's father who smiled and nodded his head in gratitude or agreement. Then, he spoke for a few minutes in English about the importance of intercultural relations between the Arab world, Spain and Latin America.

The Colombian consul, who was the bald senior executive seated next to Fardan Senior, got up, and greeted everyone in Arabic. Then, switching to English, he spoke about the need to strengthen diplomatic ties between Latin American countries and the Arab world, and of the mutual advantages that would result from it. In reference to the project Al Morsi senior mentioned, he said that a Colombian delegation was to arrive in Dubai in a few weeks to discuss it at length as well as a joint business strategy in the mining sector. In closing, he said that the museum annex in Bogotá was the beginning of a great friendship, and after a short applause, he resumed his seat.

Tony noticed that Wendy wanted to get his attention, and when he looked at her, she mouthed the word Casablanca. He smiled and nodded, indicating that he had also noticed that the consul's closing quoted Humphrey Bogart's final line in the movie. He wondered if the consul did it on purpose, meaning to be ironic perhaps, or if it was a mere coincidence. In any case, what he had just heard added a piece to the puzzle, at the center of which were the will and the documents that he translated for Fardan's father, as well as the furniture and books listed in them.

Right before he heard Fardan senior talk about the museum project, his intention to buy those pieces of furniture had been an interesting coincidence, but after hearing what he and the others said, he realized how little *he* knew about the country he was in and the interests it had in Colombia. Perhaps Al Morsi, who had just taken a seat next to him, could give him more clues, though the best source would be the Colombian consul, but he would rather not approach him. He needed to keep a low profile for as long as he could.

Tony looked at his neighbor, who seemed a little nervous or flustered; perhaps he was not pleased with his place at the table. Before he could address him, Al Morsi said something to him in Arabic, a greeting, a promise of peace. He already understood that and shook Tony's hand.

"Excuse me, but I don't speak Arabic," Tony said in English.

"My mistake," said Al Morsi. "You have a very Arabic bearing and I assumed you would speak our language."

Tony told him not to worry, and that he was used to people mistaking him for an Arab.

"Excuse my clumsiness," his neighbor went on. "Sometimes I get confused with people. May I know where you're from?"

"From the United States," Tony replied.

"My first name is Ahmed," said Al Morsi, whose face had suddenly reddened. Perhaps the issue of citizenship was something that stressed him or caused him discomfort. "I'm Egyptian, but I've been in Dubai for twenty years. I am a professor of political science and the director of the Islamic Studies program at Dubai International University; I don't know if you've heard of it."

"I've heard of it," Tony admitted. He was going to add that he knew Professor Deenik, but he decided not to. He remembered Deenik's comments about the heated debates about Al-Andalus at the university. It occurred to him that Al Morsi and Deenik might not see eye to eye on that topic.

"It's a wonderful institution, you know," Al Morsi remarked and drummed his fingers on the table. "We have a first-class faculty, graduates of the best universities, and we do a lot of research in the area, the Arab Gulf, I mean. I am myself a specialist in regional politics."

"And you're also an expert on the culture of Andalusia?" Tony asked.

"Yes, I am. Everything related to Al-Andalus fascinates me,"

Al Morsi replied and loosened his tie. The knot was very tight and he had to use both hands. "As you may know, the history of Al-Andalus is quite important to our Islamic civilization. It was a period of great achievements, in mathematics, medicine, and geography, to mention just a few. I've published a few things about it."

Tony said he understood and wanted to ask him what his publications were about, but Al Morsi spoke first and asked him whether he knew about the Muslim conquest of the Iberian Peninsula and of Islamic governance from that point forward. When Tony replied that he didn't, Al Morsi proceeded to answer the questions himself, at some length. Al Morsi spoke slowly and enunciated his words carefully; he was clearly accustomed to lecture on the topic and seemed pleased to share his knowledge. His English was fluent with a vague American accent, though at times he used odd expressions, perhaps translated directly from Arabic.

At some point, Fardan, who was listening to the conversation, told Al Morsi that Tony was helping them purchase some pieces of furniture for the cultural foundation.

"Oh, of course," commented Al Morsi. "Dr. Fardan told me about those antique furnishings. He is a true expert in Al-Andalus antiques; he has a considerable collection in his mansion in Seville, which he says is his second home. He asked me to write something about one of the pieces in particular. It seems it has decorations of religious significance. To that end, I'll have to travel to Colombia, something that has me a little worried, truth be told; it's a dangerous country, as we all know. I would have preferred to go to Al-Andalus where the pieces are likely from, although their true origin is Syrian, actually."

"Our consultant in Spain tells us that the works were probably made by artisans in Colombia in the fifteenth or sixteenth century," Fardan said and looked at Tony sideways.

"Well, though the place of manufacture is of some importance, it is not what makes them valuable," Al Morsi hastily remarked, perhaps annoyed that Fardan had interrupted his monologue. "The true value of those works is that they are part of Islamic decorative art. We must set the record straight about the origin and identity of the material culture of Al-Andalus, even in that late period…"

"Dr. Al Morsi awaits the return of Al-Andalus to our sphere of cultural and religious influence," Fardan said in his tone a trace of mockery.

"That's not what I mean," Al Morsi countered and looked at Fardan, his brow furrowed, and his face slightly blushed. "The topic of Al-Andalus is very complex and we must proceed with caution. What I meant in relation to those objects is that we must give proper credit where it is due to Islamic civilization."

"I suppose there will also be expert curators at the cultural center that will help you with that assessment," Wendy intervened in a casual tone, her eyes on the entrée a waiter had just served her.

"Of course, that goes without saying," Al Morsi replied, rather formally. "I'm told they have qualified curators at the museum. We are also hiring our own curator of Al-Andalus material culture, who will be based in Dubai and will coordinate with the center's staff in Seville and in Colombia. I'm the Chair of the search committee. Your boss, the director of the university library too; she's a very capable woman, a graduate of the University of Cairo, like me. We already have several highly qualified candidates that we'll interview soon," he continued. "I'm confident we'll find the right person who can set the right tone.

Tony noticed that Wendy and Fardan looked at each other with an air of complicity. It occurred to him that they were lovers too, but he immediately dismissed the idea. It struck him as ridiculous. Their relationship seemed more like of a teacher and student, although there was undoubtedly a bond of affection.

"But tell me, my friend, what brought you to Dubai?" Al Morsi asked Tony.

"Business opportunities," he replied and left the sentence in the air.

"Ah, business," said Al Morsi and smiled. "I envy you, my friend. In this city one can become very rich. The cost of setting up businesses in the city is very reasonable, and there are no taxes on corporate profits or personal income, not to mention the abundance of qualified labor. The main draw, however, is the political stability of the country, and the incentives for foreign investment."

Tony nodded, and decided not to say anything else. Something told him that Al Morsi was not trustworthy. Besides, he was an academic, someone who worked with abstractions and very likely had little experience in the real world.

Wendy, who was following the conversation, made a comment about the political scene in Dubai that Tony did not understand—his attention was diverted at that moment because Fardan hurriedly got up and left the table. Al Morsi replied that whatever it was western leaders, for the most part, misunderstood the Islamic world and its traditions and principles, and from that point forward, Wendy and Al Morsi moved on to a discussion on democracy and the monarchies of the Arabian Gulf, which at first Tony found interesting and entertaining. Unfortunately, after a comment that Wendy made about the role of women and religion—which made it clear that Wendy, as he, was not a believer—Al Morsi adopted a moralizing tone, which reminded Tony of some altercations with his father, who was religious and conservative and had nothing but contempt for non-believers and people who did not share his views.

To detach himself from the conversation, Tony looked around the table. He had hardly paid attention to the guests on the other side. Apart from the Colombian consul, there were four men and four women, all of them middle aged. The men in *Kandura*, the women in *Abayas* with the exception of a young blonde with Slavic features that seemed familiar to him. She was sitting almost at the end of the other side of the table, reading something on her mobile, seemingly oblivious to her surroundings. Like him, she had barely touched the food. Perhaps she wasn't hungry, or like him, didn't care for Moroccan food, though he found it tasty, even though it didn't agree with his stomach.

While looking in that direction, he noticed that a crew of five Indian or Bangladeshi workers in blue overalls were preparing a small rectangular stage next to the table. Fardan Junior gave them instructions in a low voice; perhaps they had prepared some sort of performance to go with the coffee and desert they were serving for the guests. On the other side of the table, Fardan Senior was now talking with the Colombian consul who was all smiles. They seemed comfortable with each other, as if they had been friends for a long time. The consul was likely from the Caribbean region; he had that air about him, also a glint of mischief in his eyes. He reminded him of an older cousin in the coastal city of Santa Marta where his family went on vacation during the long end of year holidays, and who taught him how to swim in the ocean. His maternal uncle and his wife had a large, old colonial house with white stucco walls a few blocks from the beach. He and his parents—his mother was still alive—slept in one of the large dark rooms facing the inner patio that had a small garden with a thick papaya tree and a bougainvillea forever in bloom that climbed over the walls. It was a distant memory. More than thirty years had passed, but he could still remember that house; the heavy dark wood furniture in the living and dining rooms, the colorful tiles of geometric design on the floors where he played with his toy cars, and the old wicker rocking chair where his mother would sit to do a bit of knitting in the long hot January afternoons.

Once the workers finished setting the stage, three musicians dressed in Levantine attire and red fez hats, two of them with lutes, the other with a *Darbuka* goblet drum, climbed onto it. After a brief tuning of the strings, the trio played a melancholic tune that increased in tempo as the young Slavic-looking blonde, the one who minutes before was at the table, now dressed in a tight fitting blouse cut above the navel and a long sheer skirt with side slits, took to the stage and started swaying to the music.

Al Morsi, attentive to what was happening, gave Wendy a quick nod, perhaps indicating the end of their conversation, crossed his arms and turned his attention to the stage. Wendy, who seemed suddenly animated texted something on her mobile and looked at Tony, indicating that the message was for him. The text read that the dancer was at the Jazz festival and was one of Fardan's girlfriends.

Tony nodded in agreement to Wendy, and looked at the young woman on the stage, who a few moments ago had seemed the person most out of place at the table, not only because she looked bored, but because she was the most foreign—or rather least Arab-looking—person there apart from Wendy. Her movements were in perfect sync with the music, and at the same time looked spontaneous and fluid, perhaps she was a professional dancer. When she shook her hips, a smile drew on her face, eyebrows raised, and her gaze went around the table focusing on each and every guest as if acknowledging their pleasure at looking at her body. At some point, beams of colored lights fell on her, and the musicians tightened the tempo, the lutes forward, one after the other, the goblet drum right behind. The young woman quickened her pace, and, from time to time, shook her head so that her mane of hair fell on her face and then again on her back. Tony found the scene unreal and out of place, as if he was watching it on a movie screen. It made him think of his club in Roppongi, which featured burlesque shows every night, and of a Russian dancer he dated for a while two or three years ago. He tried to remember the face and the name of the Russian girl, but what came to his mind was Adriana's face. He felt a sudden desire for her, for her body, her face, also her voice. He thought he would have to look for her, call her friends in Tokyo with whom she might be in touch, but right away realized that it was not a good idea; it would make him look weak and sentimental, something she detested. Besides, Adriana had betrayed *him*. It was *she* who would have to look for him and ask for forgiveness.

After a few minutes, the tempo of the music and the dance got slower, and the beams of colored lights faded. When the music came to an end, the young blonde made a quick bow and left the stage to resounding applause.

Some of the guests got up and gathered their things, Al Morsi included. Tony leaned toward Wendy and asked what she thought about the show. He was ready for some banter to chase away any thought of Adriana, but rather than answer she looked at him and arched her eyebrows, indicating that there was someone or something to his side that he should pay attention to. Tony looked around and saw Fardan Senior standing next to him.

"I wanted to personally thank you for your work," he said when they shook hands. "I hope you enjoyed the dinner and the show."

Tony nodded and blurted yes, of course, and suddenly felt nervous. He could not think of anything else to say.

"If you have time this week," Fardan Senior went on, "I would like us to meet in my office. My assistant will call you tomorrow to set a time. This evening I have to retire early, an occupational hazard, I'm afraid," he added, and bid his farewell in Arabic, another expression he already understood.

Tony nodded and said he looked forward to the meeting and shook, again, Fardan Senior's hand. He thought he was beginning to understand who was who in Dubai.

When Fardan Senior left, Wendy suggested they should go somewhere for a drink. Tony nodded his head and said it was an excellent idea, that he sure could use a double shot of tequila. On their way out, Fardan Junior joined them, saying the night is young.

SIXTEEN

The man talking to Professor Rodrigues was her grand-father, Paola thought, and felt a chill run from the crown of her head to the back of her neck; it could not be, though, her beloved Grandpa had died four months ago. She was seeing visions. She quickened her pace around the fountain of the lions, her eyes fixed on that man. With each step she could see his face better. It was an amazing resemblance. It would have to be a twin of his, a great uncle she never knew. Or was she dreaming? No, it was not that, perhaps fatigue made her see visions. She did not sleep well the night be-fore; Esteban's idea of stealing the bargueño kept her tossing and turning. Taking it out of the museum was what he said, something she was sure she was not going to do, though it might be the only solution to her problems. Later, before dawn she had several nightmares. Poorly lit scenes where she fled from someone or something; first in a house that was collapsing, then on a narrow path in a forest where she ran not knowing towards where.

When she arrived at the café, the same one where they met the first time, Rodrigues and the other man got up to greet her. Something that was odd for they could not have seen her come. She had been watching them since she entered that short wing of the mall. Did Rodrigues know it was her by the clicking of her shoes? She hated wearing heels. She would rather wear sneakers or sandals, but Esperanza told her not to; she said that as long as she worked with her at the agency, she always had to make a good impression, that is, she had to pretend in public to be something she was not.

Rodrigues said hello and shook her hand and introduced him to the man whose name he said was Robert Hendrik Deenik.

"Pleased to meet you," she said and could not help looking at him from head to toe. The resemblance was amazing; the thick hair combed back, and the long thoroughly white beard, were the same. The difference was that her grandfather had been taller and darker, and his eyes, though light colored, were gray, not blue like Deenik's.

"We came from a faculty meeting at the Abu Dhabi campus," Rodrigues said. "The university bus driver said he could drop us off at this mall from which it would be easier for both of us to get home by metro. I'm glad you were free to come see us on such short notice."

"Thank you for coming. As I mentioned in my email, I'm worried about the curators taking so long. At this point, I would like to contact the law firm that you told me about."

"Yes, of course, Paola. I'll send you the information this afternoon. It's a firm that has its main office in San Francisco, California. I wasn't sure that they worked on cases regarding artworks, so I called Miryam, my biological daughter, who is one of the main partners, and she told me they handle all kinds of cases, and that if you agree, no strings attached, without any kind of payment upfront, they could contact the museum to review the case."

"I truly appreciate this, professor," Paola said, and despite herself bowed to him Japanese style as she was taught she should to an older and well-respected customer.

"Don't mention it," Rodrigues said and lowered his head slightly. "Since we don't have much time, let me get straight to the point."

"Thanks, professor, and please accept my apology. In half an hour I have to rush to catch a bus to Abu Dhabi; it's a work-related matter."

"We understand, don't worry," Rodrigues said and looked at Deenik, who smiled and preened his beard. "Back to the *Arca de Noé*," Rodrigues went on, "Professor Deenik and I have some comments, and a new hypothesis. We both agree that Professor Cortés' theory—the Jesuit I mentioned the other day—that Maimonides was the man in the engraving is not convincing enough. From what we know and have read about his life, Maimonides didn't have a particular interest with issues related to converts or to the deluge and Noah's Ark. However, neither of us are experts in the history of the Iberian Peninsula in the Middle Ages, so you should take our comments with a grain of salt. However, we believe that what we've found so far could be useful to you in the future."

Rodrigues paused and looked at Deenik.

"At first, I thought that the man in the turban could be Isaac Abravanel, another eminent Andalusian Jewish philosopher, though from the fifteenth century not the twelfth like Maimonides," Deenik said, his right hand still on his beard. "What made me think that was a remarkable resemblance between an ink portrait of his I found in a manuscript I'm researching and the engraving in the bargueño. Although I must say that they both look alike; perhaps all bearded men of a certain age look alike…"

"Yes, it's true," Paola said, and right away felt herself blush. "I beg your pardon, professor, please go on."

Deenik nodded and smiled. "The other reason," he went on, "are some writings of Abravanel, who was a prolific writer and an intellectual. In one of the sources I consulted, I found that following the expulsion of the Jews in fourteen-ninety-two—the same year as Columbus's first trip to the New World—Abravanel wrote several political and theological works about conversion and converts, topics that I'm researching at the moment for an article that I intend to write, by the way. Apart from his great intellect, Abravanel was also very skilled in politics and finance, and thanks to that he had the favor and protection of several European notables and nobles. What I mean to say is that Abravanel was a well-respected man. Do you follow me so far?"

Paola nodded her head. She was a little nervous because Esperanza, who always helped her when she did not understand something in English, was not with her. Fortunately, Deenik spoke slowly, enunciating his words carefully, and so far, she understood everything. What added to her nerves was Deenik's resemblance to her grandfather, which had the effect of allowing images of her Grandfather Rafael to come and go through her head. Did he ever talk about this Abravanel, a name that for some reason sounded familiar to her, or about Jewish people who converted?

"Well, the other aspect of Abravanel's life that fed my suspicions," Deenik continued, "was the fact that his family dispersed across many countries. That was common in Jewish families because of the prejudice and persecutions they encountered. Some of their descendants live in the American continent, although as far as I know, mostly in the United States; we would have to see if some settled in South America. I wouldn't be surprised. But although these clues would make us think of Abravanel as that 'important figure of his faith', in the engraving, what we've found out recently could be more convincing…"

"The hypothesis we have is somewhat daring," Rodrigues said and looked at Deenik who had paused and at that moment seemed absorbed with something else, perhaps some idea that had occurred to him. He was about to go on, but Deenik indicated with his hand that he wanted to say something.

"Excuse me for stopping that way, sometimes it happens to me; I'm always tying loose ends in my head. I just remember that one of Abravanel's descendants, a professor of literature in the United States if I'm not mistaken, has written several historical novels about Jews in Spain and Portugal, and also an academic monograph in which she maintains that Christopher Columbus was a Jew. It would be prudent to take a look at the sources she used. It could shed new light on Abravanel's descendants' movements. Although as I said before, this new hypothesis is quite convincing. My apologies for the interruption Tomás. Please go on."

Rodrigues frowned and smiled at the same time. "It's something we came across by chance," he said. "We found a mention about Noah's Ark in a footnote of a text about the importance of Noah's story for the Jews as it marks the beginning of their history as a people. A subject that, incidentally, didn't allow us to doubt a Jewish link to the bargueño. The footnote was a reminder that Noah's Ark's story is common to the three Abrahamic religions, Judaism, Christianity, and Islam, and had a reference to a sixteenth century miniature painting."

"You can see that work of art here," Deenik said and handed Paola an iPad tablet that he had on the table. Paola looked at the image of the painting, which immediately caught her attention. Perhaps she had seen it before. It was a horseshoe-shaped ship, or perhaps it was a cross section of it, sailing through a storm. The water and the sky around it were a leaden blue with dark strokes like gusts of wind. At the bottom of it, there was a man dressed in red trying to get on the boat, perhaps he had fallen overboard; two men wearing turbans were trying to help him, and an alligator was threatening to bite his legs. In that part of the ship there were some animals. Amongst them, an elephant and a deer. In the compartment above, the middle one and the largest, there were other animals as well; one or two horses, a tiger, a cat, and some monkeys. In the upper deck, there was a bearded man wearing a turban, and behind his head was a golden circle as if he were a saint. That would be *Noé*, Noah, Paola thought. Above it, on the main mast, there was a man, this one without a turban, watching three or four men who were lowering a sail in what looked like the prow of the boat.

"I don't see any women," Paola said, and in that instant, she felt that she had already said that sometime in the past; perhaps it was an illustration she had seen when she was little, otherwise she would remember it better. Linked to that thought came a memory of Grandfather Rafael who often read to her from a book he kept in his room. The little book that his father mentioned the other day; perhaps she had seen this curious painting in that little book.

Rodrigues and Deenik nodded their heads and looked at each other.

"What drew our attention was Noah's drawing," said Deenik.

Paola looked again at the image to the bearded man with a turban and a golden circle behind his head.

"It's the man in the bargueño!" she cried out.

"Another important parallel are the animals," Deenik noted.

"All of them are in the bargueño engravings and appear in the same order, starting with the one to the right of Noah, following the hands of the clock."

Paola enlarged the size of the image, and again felt that she had seen that image some time ago. You are a lioness; she suddenly remembered her grandfather saying to her once. A little one for the moment, but when you grow up you will be a big one, a true *lioness*. That was what her grandfather told her. He repeated it several times in an affectionate tone on one of her birthdays; she would have been eight or nine. That day, if her memory served well, he gave her two books as a gift. Her grandfather loved her very much; nobody had given her a book before, not afterwards either. She did not remember the titles only the covers; one had a star within another star, and the other a picture or drawing of a bearded old man wearing a turban. Her mom did not like the books; she said she was too young to read them, that she would keep them for a while, and indeed she did. She put them on a glass cabinet with a lock of which she only had the key. She did not know what happened to them afterwards, more than twenty years had passed.

"The lion in the middle is smiling," Paola said.

"It's the same in the bargueño; it's the only animal that the artisan copied from this painting," Deenik noted. "The drawings of the rest are different."

"And what does it mean?"

"To begin with, it is possible as we have speculated, that the artisan copied the figures from the painting. But, most importantly, it's an Indian miniature painting from the Miskin dynasty of the Mughal period, a sixteenth century Muslim empire." Whoever commissioned it, or whoever made it, had that image. That is, had a copy of it, probably in a book printed in India, although it could have been printed somewhere else. We would have to investigate."

"The Portuguese brought the printing press to Goa, in India, a province they founded there in the sixteenth century; the same century of the painting," Rodrigues added.

"This is all very confusing," Paola said and cradled her face with her hands.

"Let's take stock of what we know so far," Rodrigues said and crossed his arms. "One, according to the curators at the museum in Bogotá, the bargueño is from the sixteenth century, although we don't know if it was made in Spain or in the New World. Two, the story of the deluge and Noah's Ark is common to at least three religions, Judaism, Christianity and Islam, though the myth of the deluge is mentioned in the Poem of Gilgamesh, an ancient Mesopotamian epic. Three, the central engraving and that of one of the animals are copied from an Indian miniature painting made during the Mogul Muslim empire in the sixteenth century. This suggests that the artisan—or whoever commissioned the bargueño—was a Muslim, but there may well be another explanation. We would have to find out whether that image was published in other books, and whether those books made it to Spain or the New World. Four, one member of the family who claims to have donated the bargueño to the museum has a Jewish Ashkenazi ancestor. Five, your family is related to the family that donated the bargueño, which suggests that your family also has a Jewish Ashkenazi ancestor. The only way to be certain at this point is with the result of your dad's DNA test."

"That someone has Ashkenazi DNA doesn't necessarily mean that the ancestor from he or she inherited it was a practicing Jew," Deenik interjected.

"How can that be?" Paola asked.

"The Iberian Peninsula was truly a melting pot of cultures and ethnic groups, and there were conversions from one religion to another for political reasons for many centuries," Deenik replied. "What we call the Ashkenazi ethnic group coalesced in the first millennium during the sacred Germanic Roman Empire along the River Rhine in Central Europe. The very word Ashkenazi is derived from Ashkenaz, the name of Noah's first grandson, by the way…"

Deenik was going to say something else, but stopped and wrinkled his forehead, as if something had suddenly occurred to him. Paola raised her eyebrows and looked at Rodrigues, who indicated that Deenik was about to go on.

"I beg your pardon," Deenik said. "It's just that a couple of weeks ago, I was talking with a young man of Colombian origin about the mixing of cultures and the Jewish diaspora…"

Paola thought she didn't hear well and looked back at Rodrigues.

"Professor Deenik has Sephardic Jewish ancestry," Rodrigues explained.

"Oh, I understand," Paola said, but she felt lost. Perhaps Deenik's phrasing in English confused her. "Excuse me, professor, didn't you say that you spoke recently with a Colombian of Jewish descent?"

"What? Oh, yes," Deenik replied. "It's a young neighbor with whom I converse from time to time. But that is not relevant, at least not for the moment. What I was going to say—and please bear in mind I'm speculating—is that some Ashkenazi might have migrated to Iberia during the time of the Muslim conquest and mixed with Sephardic Jews…"

"That would explain why descendants of Spaniards that made it to the New World carry Ashkenazi DNA in their blood," Rodrigues said.

"Although, there could be another explanation," Deenik

added. "You would have to go case by case because it is also possible that they inherited it from ancestors from other European countries where the Ashkenazi settled."

"Wow, that's complicated," Paola said.

"It is," Rodrigues conceded." Sorry to add another possibility, going back to the other hypothesis that we mentioned before, and that we can't rule out."

"Please go on."

"We can't rule out the possibility that whoever made it, or commissioned to have it made, was a Muslim."

"Do you mean that we have Arab ancestry?"

"Not necessarily," Rodrigues replied. "As Hendrik said, The Iberian Peninsula was a melting pot of cultures and people. The Muslims who settled there were of various origins; Arabs from the Levant, from the Arabian Peninsula, and also Berbers, from North Africa. But back to the issue of conversions; there were also converts to Islam, that is, Christians who converted either by force or on their own. They were called *Moriscos*."

"From the word *Moor*, which was what Christians called Muslims…"

"Wow, this is all like a puzzle," Paola lamented.

"I imagine that the museum experts will be considering all possible hypotheses," Rodrigues said. "They have more resources than we do, so you'll soon find out."

"Couldn't we do something to make it faster?"

"That your father is doing a DNA test is a very important step."

"It didn't occur to the museum administrators."

"They don't know what you know about your family's history."

"You are right, professor, we're ahead of them on that account."

"By the way, do you have a family tree of your father's family?"

"I doubt it. I never heard my grandfather, or my dad say anything about it. I have to ask. Professor, why do you think the experts are taking so long?"

"I don't know, but if they've considered the things that Hendrik and I mentioned, they would have to search through several archives. The General Archive of the Nation in Bogotá, to start. They've probably done that already. If they did not find anything useful there, they would have to look in Spanish archives, The National Historical Archive in Madrid, which has documents related to the Inquisition in Cartagena de Indias, and further, if necessary, in the General Archive of the Indies in Seville."

"The Inquisition in Cartagena?"

"If, as we suspect, one or several of your ancestors were converts, it is possible that the church investigated their background and activities in case there were doubts about the sincerity of the conversion," Deenik said, who was looking at his mobile while she and Rodrigues were talking; perhaps he received a text or some other message.

"Why in Madrid?"

"Because that's where some of those documents ended up. Many others, perhaps the bulk of it, got lost…"

"And in Seville?"

"That archive covers the period of Spanish governance in the New World," Rodrigues explained. "They could find evidence there of the migration of the ancestors of the Bogotá family, which could also be yours."

"Cartagena, Madrid, Seville," Paola murmured. "This is going to take a long time, isn't it?"

"Perhaps the San Francisco lawyers can help you streamline the process," Rodrigues said. "They are very skilled,

I assure you. They could put some pressure on the museum to complete the investigation in a timely manner."

"I hope so, professor. The truth is that I need this matter settled as soon as possible."

"I wish you luck, Paola."

"Me too," Deenik added.

"Thank you very much, professors. I appreciate you taking the time to come talk to me."

"We'll keep on it," Rodrigues said and looked at Deenik who nodded yes.

"Are you going to the metro station? The bus station is next to it. We could walk together."

"We'll stay a while longer," Rodrigues said. "We have some homework to do. We are going to take pictures of this fountain, which, according to the mall's brochure, is a replica of the Fountain of the Lions in the Alhambra, in Granada. The question is, of what period?"

"It is somewhat related to your case," Deenik added. "Everything is related, needless to say."

They are a couple of old farts, Paola thought and waved them goodbye. Before turning around, she realized there was a mirror at the back of the café. From where she was standing, she was saying goodbye to herself…

SEVENTEEN

Tony looked at himself in the bathroom mirror. He looked tired; he had dark circles under his eyes. He took off the amber tinted lenses he was wearing and turned on the water tap. He took a deep breath, inhaled, held, and then exhaled. He had to calm down. He had just seen Adriana in the banquet room! She looked different; had short platinum blond dyed hair, and wore an elegant black dress, and high heels. She looked thinner, and her face was tanned, though not by the sun, probably just makeup. He recognized her because at some point she got up to greet someone who had come to her table. If she had turned a little to her right, she would have seen him in profile and perhaps she would have recognized him, although she had never seen him with his shaven head and glasses.

He looked at his face again in the mirror and imagined a scene in which he ran into her face to face in that room. She slapped him, then hugged him, then shouted at him, told him that he had abandoned her, that he had left her to fend for herself…

He could not go back. He would go to his room at the hotel and would call Wendy to explain his sudden departure; but he had to think with a cool head what he was going to say. It was not a good idea to tell her the truth, that he left because he did not want to meet his former lover and partner, the person who had put him in the mess he was in, and who, by some coincidence, was attending that odd event.

He took his mobile out of his pocket and looked at it; he had no new messages, only the one from Vladimir that he received that morning in which he confirmed that the storm had passed, that the bosses had already recovered their investment or the profit they expected. Some newly arrived girls from Mexico had taken the place of Adriana and the other woman who ran away, so he was already free; his only punishment was exile. He could not go back to Roppongi. He could not get a job there. No one would hire him. What a coincidence it was that just today he saw Adriana. Perhaps she was also free of the *yakuza*—although Vladimir had not told him anything about it—perhaps she had paid off her debt with the inheritance she once mentioned, and was starting a new life, like him. He wondered how much it was—no doubt more than the fifty thousand dollars of the fine she was required to pay—and what kind of life she led now; given her business attire it would have to be something well paid. Adriana never dressed like that, not because she did not have the money to do it, it just was not her style, and it did not fit with her personality. Perhaps she worked for the lawyer who organized the event; she was sitting next to him, as if she were his right hand, but what kind of work would it be? The lawyer's short speech at the start, a few words of thanks for a job well done to the attending employees and to prominent Emirati leaders he did not name, but that included Fardan's family, for he was at his table with

Wendy and made a short bow when the lawyer mentioned that. It did not add anything to what Wendy had told him; it was a private celebration of the end of a contract of mostly soldiers and officers of the Colombian army who worked for a security company based in Dubai. It would be the end of a multi-year contract; the soldiers and officers with some exceptions were there with their wives and children. Wendy would know more about it. At some point when he was talking to Fardan, she went to the other table where moments later he saw Adriana, and spoke for a few minutes with another woman, whom he saw in profile and thought could be Colombian. She had a family resemblance to Adriana; it was probably the Colombian woman that Wendy had told him was the owner of a modeling agency. Maybe Adriana worked with her, not as a model or hostess but in some administrative capacity.

In the hotel room, he made himself a gin and tonic and sat in an armchair by the window overlooking the sea. In the distance was Abu Dhabi downtown; you could see some skyscrapers and apartment towers on a smaller scale than in Dubai and were more uniform and sedated. They were on one of the islands that surrounded the city in the same touristic area as the Formula One race track and the Ferrari theme park, which were literally a killing combination; speed was a public health problem in the country as the death rate due to traffic accidents was very high.

But what was he thinking? He had just seen Adriana, the woman with whom he had lived for more than a year, with whom, despite their differences, he had planned to live with in the future, though they had never made any real plans… It was ironic that he had once imagined Adriana in Dubai in one of the glass clad condominiums facing the sea; it was a fantasy, that only differed from reality as far as the city. Adriana was in Abu Dhabi!

Tony got up and walked in circles around the room. Having seen Adriana changed things in some way; in what way, he didn't know, though it added one more piece to the puzzle that his life in that desert exile had become.

On the way from Dubai to Abu Dhabi in Fardan's SUV, he had felt at peace. He had thought that despite all the questions he had about his new job—the one-year contract as a cultural consultant Fardan's father had offered him—his life was taking a new and different course that was somehow more desirable than it had in Japan. To his mind came the brief meeting with Fardan's father in his office on the top floor of a skyscraper in Dubai International Financial Center where he made him the offer to work with his son on the matter of the artworks and the Cultural Center, and on other related projects that may come up. It was an offer that he had happily accepted; the salary that Fardan Senior offered him was almost double of what he earned at the Sonatine. His relationship with Wendy had also moved forward and in an important way; they had agreed to live together at Wendy's apartment, though he would keep his own place. After all, it came with his job and it was not his to give up. The news from Vladimir that morning had been the icing on the cake, so to speak, to the beginning of his new life. To close the chapter of his life in Tokyo, he would ask his friend Pablo, the Peruvian journalist to whom he had entrusted the keys of his apartment, to sell his furnishings and do the necessary paperwork to end his lease. He would call him as soon as he had some time alone. As way of payment, he could tell him about the Colombian soldiers in the Emirates so he could finish the piece on Latin Americans expatriates in Asia he was working on.

Back in the armchair, Tony thought that perhaps he had been wrong to return to the room. Although his work with

Fardan had not formally started—they had not yet discussed the particulars, such as the schedule and working hours—he had the impression that accompanying him to tonight's event was part of what was expected of him. The invitation came through Wendy, who just told him that Fardan had asked her if the two of them could go with him to Abu Dhabi that weekend, that they would stay at one of the new Yas Island hotels, and that they would attend a social event on Saturday night on behalf of his father who had to travel to Kuwait on an urgent business matter. What was the link of this event with Fardan's family business? He had the feeling that Fardan himself did not know; when he asked on the way to Abu Dhabi, Fardan laughed and said that they would find out on the fly, and that his father had only told him he had to make an appearance, or that nobody was going to ask him or demand anything from him. Perhaps Fardan's father was one of those businessmen who expect those who work for him to figure out on their own how things are done, and take the initiative when circumstances demand it. In Tokyo, in the business world he knew, things were also like that. It occurred to him that tonight's event was just a gesture of gratitude towards those soldiers and whoever contacted and hired them to work for the security company.

But to secure what? The government, the sheikhs in power? The ports of entry to the country? Important works of infrastructure, the electrical grid, the pipelines, the refineries? From what he saw in the room, the military personnel, the mercenaries, really, were veterans mostly in their thirties and forties. It was interesting that they were there, though somehow unexpected. But it was not surprising because with the end of armed conflict in Colombia, many members of the armed forces were rendered inactive, perhaps with a notable reduction in income, especially those with advanced training. But it was a subject that he didn't know much about. He didn't follow Colombian news; from time to time, he took a look at the headlines of online Bogotá dailies, and only took a closer look in case of some sporting victory, a stage or race win in cycling or a good result in a football game. Sports he only had a superficial interest in but that in some way tied him it to the country, a sort of sport patriotism. His main source of information was the Japanese national news network, online or on television—he got it through the cable service—or one of the Japanese online newspapers whose opinion columns he diligently read in Japanese.

As a sort of reflex, he opened his computer and searched for information on Colombian mercenaries in the United Arab Emirates. The search engine yielded several articles; two from Colombian newspapers and one from a New York daily, though they were reports from three or four years ago, nothing current, and their content was more or less the same; the recruitment and training initially through an American security company, then directly by the UAE army. Most suggestive in one of the pieces he read that some Colombian mercenaries were fighting in Yemen, a neighboring country in the middle of a civil war, but it was also an old story from two years before, and there was no follow up to that.

He was about to close his computer when his mobile rang. It was Wendy. He told her he had a bit of an upset stomach and had already had a glass of water with salts for indigestion and would return in a matter of ten or fifteen minutes. Wendy told him she understood and that she would update Fardan.

Unexpectedly, perhaps by suggestion or coincidence, he felt that, in fact, he had a touch of indigestion, and just as he told Wendy, he went to the bathroom and had a glass of water with salts for indigestion; he had the medication in his toiletry bag. Through the window overlooking the sea, he spotted a patrol boat in the distance. Its blue siren light was on; perhaps it was an emergency. Otherwise, it was a moonless night, and there were no clouds in the sky.

After a few minutes his stomach felt better, but he suddenly felt desolate, as if his life from one moment to the next was empty, meaningless; it was something he had never felt before. What was he doing with his life? He went to the bathroom, splashed water on his face, and scanned it from top to bottom; it was a new habit for him, perhaps because he felt older and the passage of time began to bear on him. He noticed some wrinkles at the corner of his eyes and a sunspot on his cheek; the sun in Dubai was unforgiving. He would have to buy sunscreen and a good hat. He looked in Wendy's travel bag; she had told him that her skin was very sensitive, and she used a Japanese cream that worked very well. He fumbled a little in her make-up bag and saw a small container with a Japanese label that said it removed sunspots. When he opened it, he detected a perfumed scent; it was not a product he would be able to use as perfumes and strong smells in general annoyed him.

Next to the Japanese cream, there was a prescription bottle for a medication that she obviously took; the label had her name on it, although he had never seen her take it, and she never mentioned it. Maybe she was embarrassed by it. It occurred to him that it could be a tranquilizer. Wendy was sometimes a little neurotic, and had a tendency to overthink things and worry too much about them, even small matters like whether she expressed herself well or made a good impression with people whom she had just met and perhaps would never see again, things that were unimportant to him, but worried her. It sometimes even prevented her from having a good night's sleep.

On the internet he found that the medication was indeed a tranquilizer, though the dose that Wendy took was low; perhaps it was temporary. The expiration date, he noted, was in a few months. Upon returning the medication to where he found it, he felt, perhaps for the first time, a genuine concern for Wendy's health and well-being. It was obvious—he realized then—that he cared about what happened to her; he didn't want her to worry too much about anything or be distressed in any way. Was this evidence that he was falling in love with her? He looked at himself in the mirror once again, as if he could find the answer there. And what about Adriana? Did he love her or not? Who did he love more—or who did he really love, Adriana or Wendy? Perhaps what he felt for each one was different. Adriana was not fragile or sensitive like Wendy who was also an open book; she never hid or repressed anything, and her emotions were always on the surface. Adriana didn't worry too much about things. She was a strong woman, accustomed to a hard life; her reaction to difficult situations was to tackle them directly, sometimes with anger; she would rather curse out loud than cry or feel depressed about it…

With those thoughts in mind—that had served as a sort of balm for the desolation he had felt only a few minutes before—he returned to the banquet room which had an odd location. It wasn't part of the hotel where they stayed, though it was next to it on a passageway that linked the hotel with a shopping center. He recalled that the place had a back entrance that led to a pedestrian walk, which he had seen that afternoon when they arrived, and decided that he would go there; he didn't want to attract attention to himself or let Adriana see him enter by himself, unaccompanied. He had not given it another thought about what he would say to her; he would leave that to fate. It was useless to prepare for something like that, especially because Adriana was unpredictable; she could either slap him hard and shout obscenities at him, or completely ignore him and not say a word. Her situation was different now, from what he could see. She didn't need him…

In the back of the room, he saw four men who before he left sat at table next to his—it was the only table with single men—with musical instruments for *vallenato* music; an accordion, acoustic guitar, a small set of drums, and a *guacharaca* percussion, a piece of bamboo hollowed with grooves. They seemed to be about to play, though there were no microphones or sound system—the room was a really a commercial space—suitable for a small business, a fashion store, or something like that, he thought. The man with the accordion suddenly said, *here we go*. Perhaps he already introduced himself and his colleagues and began playing the first chords of a song he knew; it was one of Adriana's favorites, about a man who dedicates a song to a married woman. Perhaps Adriana had requested that song. After all she was seated next to the person who organized the event. After a few seconds, came one of the lines in the song Adriana liked to hum; it said:

> *You've got to understand that love has*
> *no bounds. There is nothing that can stop*
> *it. And, if you are the woman that moves*
> *me, I'll respect the man who calls you*
> *yours, but I must then tell you…*

Tony closed his eyes for a moment and remembered one night when he danced to that song with Adriana, though reluctantly; he didn't like that kind of music, and neither did he enjoy couple dancing. He never did that. He wasn't used to it; but Adriana begged. She told him that it was something very special for her, something that touched her soul, and asked him not to disappoint her, so he agreed and let Adriana guide him; she danced very well, and knew how to deal with a clumsy partner. Later on, they had made love and she played the song back—they were at her place—and for some reason, he memorized some lines that came later; he opened his eyes just as they began, as if he had memorized the rhythm and the timing of the song;

> *The truth is that I feel jealous when I
> see you arrive with the man who is your
> husband, and I know well that you're there
> with him because of some prejudice, even
> though you want to be with me…*

It was a part of the song that he didn't understand well at first. The business about prejudice sounded strange to him; he didn't understand what the *prejudice* was or who suffered from it, whether it was he or she. Adriana had laughed at him, a sarcastic laugh, he remembered. She told him that this was proof that *he wasn't as Colombian* as she was, or that perhaps he wasn't Colombian at all. He didn't remember exactly, but it led to an argument about his national identity, something he had never given serious thought, and he, although somewhat offended, chose not to defend himself. He said that indeed it was so, that perhaps he was no longer Colombian, he had forgotten how to be, or perhaps never had been, an argument or explanation that made Adriana laugh again, but no longer with sarcasm, just a good natured laugh, but perhaps tinged with pity. *Pobrecito,* poor little one, she'd said, and so for a whole week she told him every time she saw him. *Poor little Tony,* she'd say, *he doesn't know how to be Colombian.* Now that he thought about that incident, he realized how absurd his reaction had been. Adriana was right; he was not Colombian, or rather he was only half-way Colombian because his parents were and he'd lived in Colombia for several years, but not because he felt one hundred percent Colombian, except for sporting events, of course…

Even though his eyes were open, he did not notice Adriana dancing with the lawyer next to their table; other diners did the same. There wasn't a dance floor, or a spot that was not carpeted so people could dance. Some couples danced with their young children. They took them by the hand, and taught them how to dance, to enjoy the music and follow the beat. Despite being an innocuous, family-type scene, he thought it rather pathetic; in the faces of the couples he saw despair or disappointment, perhaps also self-denial. The lawyer who organized the event was probably Adriana's lover; they danced very close to each-other, Adriana hugged his back as if she were making love to him. Contrary to what the song suggested, or the lines he knew by heart, which they were going over just then, he didn't feel an ounce of jealousy, though it was possible that his state of mind would not allow it. It was the opposite; he thought a moment later; he was happy that Adriana had a partner just as he had his. Besides, even if it were not so, he had no right to expect anything from Adriana. He had no reason to feel jealous; they had never formalized anything. They had never promised anything to each other, much less being faithful to one another. He looked towards Wendy and Fardan. The two talked animatedly. Perhaps they were making jokes about the musicians or about the couples dancing.

He would go back to his seat. He would tell Fardan what Wendy had probably already told him, that he had a stomach upset, but that he was feeling better. He would also tell him about *Vallenato* music, its origin and history, things he had learned here and there, many of them from Adriana, who was a fan of Colombian popular music.

EIGHTEEN

Paola got an email from Sara Ruiz, the art historian:
Dear Adriana Paola,

Your mom suggested that I write to you. As you may already know, I am a historian from Bogotá, and I work at a university in Madrid. I am a descendant of the person who donated the Arca de Noé to the Museo del Virreinato. When one of the curators at the museum wrote to tell me that he had seen the photos you sent of the bargueño that you inherited from your grandfather with the engraving of the bearded man wearing a turban, I realized it could be a twin of the one my great grandfather donated to the museum.

When I travelled to Colombia a few months ago, I got in touch with your parents, and as you know, I went to your home to talk to them and look at the other bargueños. Upon my return to Bogotá, the museum asked me to be part of the team of experts in charge of the assessment of the large bargueño. As you well know, the most notable difference is the engraving on the center plate. The team initially agreed with Professor Cortes' hypothesis that the man in the engraving was Maimonides, a Jew-

ish scholar of the Middle Ages. But what Professors Rodrigues and Deenik suggest seems more convincing because of the remarkable resemblance between the engraving and the drawing of the prophet Noah in the Indian miniature painting. That the drawing and the engraving of the tigress are also similar seems to confirm this.

What surprised us most, however, was that the bargueño you inherited has two pieces of ornamental woodwork with geometric patterns that are slightly damaged in one of the side walls which belong to the one in the museum. The four pieces of woodwork are about the same age, which suggests they are twin bargueños, and whoever made the change—we don't know who it could be as there are no clues in the museum's archive—had the two bargueños in his or her possession, at least for that one time. Up to this point we were willing to state that bargueño was an antique from the seventeenth century. However, when we examined one of the tortoise shell plates on top, which we had to remove, we realized that the whole length of wood in which it was embedded was not as old as the rest of it. We ran a lab analysis of it and found that it was from the end of the nineteenth century or the beginning of the twentieth century.

When the museum's board of directors read our report, they decided, following the new standards of curatorship, that they could not attribute it to the same artist or to the same period. Although this somewhat diminishes the value of the piece, it is still quite valuable. The consultants who appraised its value in the international antiques market say that it could be worth approximately sixty thousand dollars. Unfortunately, the museum board of directors concluded that the bargueño is part of their collection, based on a nineteen-fifty document that states that two bargueños of the same size were added to the museum's collection donated by the Ruiz Valenzuela family of Bogotá. I understand that the board of directors have not found an official record or a technical file of the second bargueño in their archives, so I don't believe that their arguments will hold before a judge in court. That notwithstanding, the fact that the Ministry of Culture is in charge of the museum is likely to delay any legal proceedings; the bureaucracy in Colombia always moves at a snail's pace.

But we may have a solution at hand. This morning, I met one of the lawyers of the firm that represents you in Bogotá who told me what your father knew about your great grandfather. That is, that he suffered from a rare disease that affected his heart, which may be the key that might help us sort this out soon because it could be the same genetic disease that has affected my family for several generations. I am aware that what I am going to tell you may upset you but given the circumstances we have no choice.

I should start from the beginning. The results of your father's DNA test were quite useful because they suggest that we, you, your father and I and my father's side of the family, may be blood relatives. This is consistent with what your father said about your great-grandfather marrying a woman of the Valenzuela family—who could be my great-grandmother—after his first wife died. Even so, we cannot be completely sure due to the distance between generations. To confirm the relationship beyond any doubt, we would need a sample of your grandfather's DNA, so your family would have to exhume his body. The lawyer will call your dad this afternoon. I tell you this to give you the heads up, so you have time to think about it. If all goes well, I mean, if your dad agrees to exhume your grandfather, and the results of the DNA analysis are conclusive, the lawyer says that if we add the curatorial report of the bargueño to it, it would be enough to neutralize the museum's board of directors objections, and you would be free to sell it or do with it whatever you want.

As I told your dad a few days ago, I could buy the

bargueño for sixty thousand dollars. I am aware that you could get a better price at an auction, though there is no guarantee of it; auctions are unpredictable. I don't know if you know, but there is another interested party, Ahmad Al Morsi, a well-known Egyptian scholar who has written about the history of Andalusia, the Spanish region where the taracea, the artisanal technique to make the bargueños that your grandfather learned from his father, was developed.

Incidentally, Professor Al Morsi's ancestors come from the of Murcia Region (Morsi: from Murcia), which borders Andalusia; the expulsion of the Jews and Muslims from Spain between the fifteenth and seventeenth centuries, forced many of them to settle in new lands. In any case, when things begin to clear up, Professor Al Morsi will probably contact you to make you an offer. By coincidence, I have learned that he is a visiting professor at Dubai International University, so you may have the opportunity to meet him in person. A rumor I heard recently is that Al Morsi would make the purchase on behalf of a Dubai sheikh who has an impressive collection of Mudéjar art in Seville. If you're interested, I could dig deeper into the rumor and find out more. I have friends in Dubai that make it their business to know about such things. The museum could also make you an offer, but I doubt that it is a sum greater than the appraisal of the experts.

My interest in this bargueño is part of my search, for several years now, about the true origin of my family. When I was little, I heard my grandmother say several times that, despite what my grandfather put in our family tree, there were Jewish ancestors on his side of the family, which was a great shame for her. She was a devout Catholic from a blue blood Bogotá family. Truth be told, my grandparents did not get along; they hardly tolerated each other. My own father inherited my grandmother's prejudices and never told me what he knew of his family's origin.

Once I became a historian, I began, little by little, to dig into the history of my family, though with little success I must confess. From what I have been able to find out in several Spanish archives, my paternal family—and perhaps yours as well—are descends from Jewish converts who traveled from Spain to the New World, to Cartagena de Indias, in fifteen-forty.

I tell you all this because I have decided to write a book about my family's history and the inheritance you received from your grandfather, and I would like to ask for your help. Would you agree to an interview? From what your parents tell me, your grandfather talked a lot with you, and perhaps he told you something that would give us clues about the history of the bargueño you inherited. Depending on how much information I can gather, it could be a scholarly monograph, or perhaps a non-fiction novel. If you are willing to help me, we could talk by Skype. In any case, I believe it would be a book that would help us. That's it for the moment. My apologies for the long email.
Cordially,
Sara

Paola sat on the sofa in the living room and felt overwhelmed. She held her head with her hands and despite herself her eyes filled with tears. That the museum insisted that the bargueño belonged to them seemed cruel and inhuman. She thought of calling Esperanza. Her cousin had the knack of reading her moods and of giving her words of encouragement and comfort when she needed them, though she was surely busy with the arrangements of yet another event Esteban was organizing for the Colombian soldiers who apparently were called at the last minute to remain in the country. She would have to wait until later in the evening, after the event. She herself was riding to Abu Dhabi with Esteban in the afternoon, but she was not going to tell him anything—at least not for the time being. She needed to have a cool head and do the right thing; her future and that of her family was at stake.

She calmly reread Sara Ruiz's email. On a second reading, she thought that it was mostly good news. She remembered that Grandfather Rafael had told her several things in some of the letters he wrote that she didn't understand and that her parents couldn't either. Perhaps there was some clue there. She had to read them again. She went to her room and took her large suitcase from her bedroom closet, and at the bottom of it she found the plastic bag where she kept them. When she took the letters out of the bag, she realized that they were more numerous than she remembered. There were at least twenty; the old man wrote to her every week. She chose the last one dated in November of last year when she had just finished paying her debt to the *yakuza*. Grandfather Rafael's handwriting was large and pretty. The first time she saw it, her grandfather told her that his father taught him to write like that, in the style of a king. What else did he tell her then? Ah, that his father also taught him to draw, and to engrave on bone plates with a burin. She didn't know what a burin was, so her grandfather showed her one, a tool with a narrow sharp face at the tip, which he said he had made from a file, which was another word she didn't know, and her grandfather had burst out laughing. She would have been ten or eleven at the time, and it was a distant memory.

She read the letter, of which she remembered nothing. It was typical of her grandfather. It began with a warm greeting: *Leoncita,* he wrote. *Everything is the same in this town. As I've always said, you can sleep standing up at the main square of pure boredom.* Then, came a paragraph where he told her about her father's taxi crash that prompted the financial crisis they were facing. *I'm going to sell a few things,* he wrote a few lines below.

For that, I have to go to Bogotá, to the antique store owned by the sisters I always told you about; the ones who always bought the little frames I used to make, which they sold to their blue blood clientele at great profit—those scoundrels are very crafty. I'm sure they'll buy them for a good price; they are authentic antiques, made by your great grandfather when he was young. Today, I am going to call my great friend Dr. Carrizosa, Doctorcé, I call him. I've already told you about him. We've known each other since we were children in the Las Nieves *neighborhood. He was a very important man back in the day; he was a distinguished surgeon, a graduate of Bogotá's Universidad Nacional, and also a published poet and a thirty-third degree Mason. The poor guy can hardly walk. He fractured his hip a few years ago. He lives in a fancy downtown apartment with a housekeeper and nurse who take loving care of him. If all is well, I'll stay with him until the antiquarians pay me in cash.*

I imagine that you may be thinking that I am going to sell the treasure that I have saved for you, but don't you worry; I'm only taking two little wooden crosses with inlaid bone and tortoiseshell plates and a silver Christ, which I have long kept in the hiding place that you know of in my room. The largest one has a 'drop of oil' emerald at the base which makes it very valuable. They belonged to my mother, your great grandmother, who died young; I must have been eight or nine years old. Doctorcé remembers her; in his apartment he has photos of us when we were kids. In some of those photos you can also see our moms who were very close friends. They loved each other very much. Oh, my, this letter has made me melancholic. I send you a hug and a kiss.

As if by reflex, Paola kissed the letter and whispered, goodbye grandpa. She didn't remember seeing those wooden crosses with a silver Christ at home; the old man must have had them well hidden. One day her grandfather showed her what he kept in an old trunk he called his hiding place, but she only saw some slightly damaged books, an old robe that looked like a monk's habit, and a wooden chest where he kept some strands of hair of his mother and of him as a child, and some of the teeth that he had lost over the years.

Grandpa's teeth! They could take a DNA sample from them!

Paola put her hands to her face and blurted out, "my darling old man, may you rest in peace." She had to call home right away, though she had to wait a few hours; it would be five in the morning in Colombia.

Elated, Paola looked for another of her grandfather's letters; it occurred to her that the last one could contain another clue. The day she received it, she read it quickly, without paying attention to the details; it was the day she decided to leave Japan, the day she began her new life. That was the letter where her grandfather told that he was bequeathing her the bargueños that he had stored in the San Benito room of their home with instructions to remove the covers he had put on and to clean them a little, and then take them to Museo del Virreinato where they would issue a certificate of authenticity so they could sell them. Paola rummaged through the plastic bag and couldn't find it, though she immediately remembered that she had kept it in the handbag where she kept her personal documents; her passport, her Colombian national ID Card, her Japanese residence card, and her Emirates residence card.

Once she found the letter, she read it without haste and confirmed that she had understood everything and had followed her grandfather's instructions. She was going to put the letter back in the envelope when she realized that there was something written on the back of the last page. It was a postscript, a long paragraph that covered nearly half a page. Perhaps she didn't see it the day she read the letter for the first time because when she reached the end, where her grandfather told her that he loved her very much and said goodbye, she could not contain the tears and put the letter aside.

She read the postscript aloud, "if you have any problems with the certificate of authenticity, or if there is any doubt about the origin of any of the bargueños, you should go to my great friend, Doctorcé, that is Dr. Manuel Carrizosa Vásquez. As I told you before, we've been friends since childhood, and I trust him completely. In case he has passed, you should look for Gabriel, his eldest son, who is a great lawyer, and also a historian. Doctorcé and Gabriel know the story of the three bargueños, which I rightfully own; they are my father's inheritance with which I learned the craft. The largest is the oldest and most valuable and is the work of a distant ancestor. My dad, who liked riddles, told me that in that bargueño was the story of our family and also that of many Colombians. To my great sadness, after he gave me the bargueños, I never saw him again; his second wife forbade him to visit me; I think I told you that sometime ago. There are many other things that I couldn't tell you about my life and my family; some because they were secrets that I was forced to keep, others because I only knew bits and pieces, and therefore couldn't be sure. At this point in my life, I look to the past and realize that it is full of questions without answers. That is all. I have no more strength left. I'll see you down the road. A hug and a kiss."

NINETEEN

Tony asked the taxi driver, a middle-aged Nepalese man, if there was a café or restaurant in the neighborhood, and he told him that there were several; some behind the residential towers, along a promenade that stretched for several kilometers, and others in a square in front of the metro station they had just passed. Tony gave him a good tip. He had taken him exactly where he needed to go with minimum information; what Wendy told him in passing when she mentioned the Colombians from the modeling agency. It was a coincidence she said that; they were coming home from Abu Dhabi, stuck at a traffic jam on the highway right in the area where he was now, in the Marina district. Wendy made a comment about Fardan's platonic love for the Colombian director of the modeling agency who lived in a building owned by his family's conglomerate. She pointed her hand towards the left, though it was hard to guess where exactly; there were dozens of towers in that area and they all looked more or less the same. Fardan bragged that he always managed to find out where the girls he liked lived. When Tony got into the taxi, doubtful of whether the vague directions would be enough, the taxi driver told him not to worry, and that he knew exactly where he wanted to go. There was only one tower by that construction conglomerate in that neighborhood.

The building had a design similar to Wendy's. It was about twenty stories high, a façade of blue-tinted glass, and on top in a kind of cap on the roof terrace, was Fardan's family commercial logo with the letter F in a Gothic calligraphy font. The lobby was almost identical to Wendy's building with oversized leather furniture and large mirrors. Tony asked the doorman, an Arab man, maybe Egyptian who wore a blue uniform from a security company, if two young women, one of them with the last name Ruiz, lived there. He nodded his head yes and picked up his desk phone, perhaps to call them to say they had a visitor. Tony felt distressed; he had not thought about what to do if that happened. I just wanted to leave them a message; you don't need to call, he hastened to say, and took from his backpack a notebook and a pen to write the message, which he decided on the go would be just a brief thanks for her agency's excellent service. Below the text, he wrote in capital block letters like the rest of the message, in case Adriana recognized his handwriting, the name Ahmed; it was the first thing that came to mind. The doorman took the message and wrote sixteen-o-nine on it, probably the apartment number. Before leaving, he asked the doorman what time the young women usually left for work. He replied that they should be out any minute now and he could wait for them in the lobby if he wished. Tony felt a void in his stomach and muttered he was in a hurry, and that the message was enough.

Just as the taxi driver indicated, there was a café in the square in front of the metro station. It was possible that

Adriana and her cousin went to the office by car, in which case he would not be able to see them, but it was well worth the wait and he had no important work to do back at the office. They didn't require his presence until closing time in the evening. Although he previous night he did nothing but think about an encounter with Adriana, he still did not know exactly what he would say. He could not get used to the idea that she was in Dubai, and was someone that Wendy knew, albeit superficially. Wendy had only told him that the young woman who was dancing with the lawyer worked with Esperanza, the Colombian manager of the modeling agency.

As soon as they served the cappuccino he ordered, he saw Adriana crossing the square. She looked elegant, like the night before; she wore a cream-colored business dress and had her platinum blond hair in a bun, something that gave her a peculiar air, like a character in a Hitchcock movie. He left the café and saw Adriana enter the elevated metro station. He walked in a hurry, but when he reached the entrance the elevator had just closed its doors. He climbed the long staircase; the escalators were under repair, and when he reached the platform the signal sounded that the doors of the metro cars would close in a few seconds. He looked everywhere and saw Adriana entering the car for women and children. Although the next car was full of office employees, mostly Indian and Pakistani men, he managed to get in and carve a space for himself by the door. In each of the stations he had to get off to make sure that Adriana was still in the passenger car; from where he was, he couldn't see her.

At the Dubai Mall Station, he saw that Adriana had gotten off and was about to get on the set of moving walkways that connected the metro station with the mall. He rushed towards her, but there was a group of Asian tourists, perhaps

Chinese, who were orderly getting on the moving walkway and he had to lag behind. He navigated among the group of tourists the best way he could until he was a few meters behind her, though there were two couples in-between who ignored his request to let him pass. From where he was, he heard Adriana talk on her mobile. At some point, she raised her tone, and in English said, "I need to sign those documents as soon as possible. I have some outstanding debts in Tokyo." He thought it was not a good time to interrupt her; he would wait until she finished her call, which probably had to do with her inheritance, unless she was able to get the fifty thousand dollars she owed the *yakuza* in Tokyo during her short stay in Dubai.

In the following stretches of the moving walkway where Tony kept the same distance—the two couples still between them—Adriana continued with her call, though she only occasionally said, yes, no, okay, and of course. To pass the time, Tony turned his gaze to the different spots that tourists around him took pictures of with their mobiles. Seen from the long elevated walkway that had panoramic views of the new urban development around the Burj Khalifa tower, next to the shopping mall, the city was a geometric spectacle of steel and glass buildings of various shapes, heights and colors with novel and unusual façades that altogether fit with the commercials of brand name apparel, and lifestyles, projected on large flat-screen TVs throughout the passageway; an amazing coordination of architecture and commerce.

In the mall, he kept a longer distance between them. He noticed that Adriana was wearing cream-colored shoes—the same tone as her dress—that had thick square heels, which produced a sharp clapping sound against the marble floors. He had never seen her wear shoes like that; as a matter of fact, he had never imagined Adriana would ever dress like that. In Tokyo, she always wore jeans and knee high, high-heeled leather boots or sneakers. He wished he could see her face to face, to make sure that she was indeed the Adriana he knew, and not one of the dozens of women who walked around dressed like her in brand name apparel, perhaps also pretending to be others with pasts they wanted to leave behind once and for all.

Suddenly, Adriana finished her call and looked around, as if trying to orientate herself. Tony thought that perhaps she had a date or meeting to go to and told himself that it was time to approach her, but something within him held him back; he felt a kind of sudden panic. It seemed to him that there were too many people around, and the sound of their voices were too loud, and, besides, he didn't see any place where they could have some privacy. Meanwhile, Adriana hastened her step and he momentarily lost sight of her among a group of Asian tourists, perhaps the same ones who had blocked his way minutes ago, led by a middle-aged woman who carried a little yellow flag in her hand. Once the group made their way towards one of the food halls, he saw Adriana again, or a woman who was wearing a cream-colored dress and matching thick heeled shoes and who was going to a French department store. He had been there several times with Wendy who liked to window-shop through the different sections, especially home decor and cooking, though she never bought anything; she didn't even look at the prices.

In the luggage section, Adriana picked a wheeled suitcase that was on sale and took it to the cashiers to pay for it. Tony thought that was the right time for an encounter. He would talk to her when she was done paying; he would tell her that he had seen her by chance, and that it was an extraordinary coincidence that they met in Dubai, of all places.

On the other hand, he could wait a little longer; what he heard Adriana say about some documents no doubt related to money that she was to receive, coupled with the purchase she just made, suggested that she was preparing a trip, perhaps back to Tokyo for a few days to pay off her debt. And then return to Dubai? That would be the logical thing to do, though he couldn't be sure. Appearances were often deceiving. It was better to wait a little longer, he decided. If he continued following her, he might find out what she was up to. He needed to know.

When Adriana left the department store with her new luggage in tow, he followed her stealthily. After a few steps, he felt a kind of déjà vu, as if he had already lived that moment with Adriana, and instantly remembered that it was the other way around. It was not he who followed Adriana; she followed him. She confessed that to him the first night they spent together. She told him that it happened the night she went to look for him at his club—before they actually met; she had heard of him through the grapevine—to propose that he hire a Brazilian dancer she managed; her first underling since she paid off her own debt to one of Shinjuku's *yakuza* bosses. According to her, she was talking to the club's Nigerian doorman to whom she had asked to call him because she had some business she needed to discuss, just when he was leaving in a bit of a hurry. The Nigerian was about to call him, but she told him not to bother, that she would catch up with him on the street, and that had been her intention. But, on the way, she decided that she would wait a bit. She thought it best to watch what he was going to do perhaps in that way she would be able to tell whether he was worthy of her trust—or something along those lines; Adriana had not been convincing with her explanation. She followed him, first to an ATM where he got cash, then through several blocks to a small Latino club run by an old Venezuelan hippie, whom she knew since she arrived in Tokyo. Luckily, Tony had gone there to meet with a journalist, and sat with him at a table by the door. She sat on the other side at the bar, and had a long chat with the Venezuelan—whose name was César, and was very gossipy—and he told her things about Tony; that he was an odd guy, very dedicated to his work and didn't deal with anyone he didn't know, and that he was single and didn't have many friends, male or female. That night they did not speak, but the next, when Adriana returned to César's bar, around midnight—he had told her that Tony was coming and at what time. After observing him for a while from a table she shared with the Brazilian dancer, she went to the bar where he was having a beer and talking with César, and told him that she had heard him speak in the accent of his country, and they talked about this and that with no mention of any business, and after a while they both realized they liked each other, and that had been the beginning of their relationship. Now that *he* was following her, they were on the verge of ending what they had begun that night.

Along with that memory came to mind the scene of Adriana dancing with the lawyer in Abu Dhabi as well as the lyrics of that *vallenato* song the amateur musicians played, and the line he didn't understand that far away day when he danced with her, and that for Adriana—perhaps meaning it, or perhaps in jest—was proof that he was not as Colombian as she was or as she thought he should be. Adriana's reaction had surprised him, still surprised him, as if the question of nationality was something sacred and solemn that could only be spoken of with precision and certainty; as if the world wasn't full of people like him who had been born in one country, then lived in another one, and then in yet another one, and whose everyday conversations were mostly in his second and third languages rather than his first. How curious it was that question about nationality that some people took so seriously, and often mistook for that of citizenship. It was the first thing people said or asked when they met a stranger, and whose reply added substance and truth to the questions or comments that followed about his or her role in the grand machinery of the world. It was commonplace. People usually referred to it without problems, without hesitation, though for him it wasn't the case, with the exception of legal matters or border crossings, where what ultimately mattered was the U.S. passport he carried, with the Colombian one securely hidden in a safe place. He always hesitated as to what to say if the question was of nationality; he would look closely at whoever was asking, trying to understand or find the reason for the question, and guess the reaction to his answer. If it was an older Japanese man, he didn't hesitate to say that he was American; it bored him to talk about the country where he was born, of which he knew little these days, and of which he mostly had distant and bad memories, or to attempt to explain with what little he remembered from his high school education its lack of economic development, or its violent culture, narratives that circulated in the Japanese media and people digested without further ado. For him, in that case, the question was vitiated by a morbid desire to understand people who were poor, violent, and underdeveloped. On other occasions, especially if it was a young Japanese woman he thought he could seduce, he would say he was Spanish; the Japanese media were generous with Spain, a virile and fertile land of bulls and sun, and with a respectable average income per capita, but not as high as in Japan, of course. Moreover, his swarthy complexion and lightly hooked nose often led to bizarre doubts and confusions. Depending on where he was traveling, he could be of many nationalities; Syrian, Palestinian, Israeli, Spanish, Greek. People always took him to be this or that, and almost no one guessed his background. Even Colombians doubted him. They would tell him they would have never guessed it, and that he didn't have the air or the accent. Years ago, in Lisbon, one of his favorite cities, a Turkish man in a restaurant told him that he was sure that he was Kurdish because of his facial features, and that he knew well that he held a grudge against his fellow compatriots; it was an unpleasant encounter where he was almost physically attacked, this time saved by his passport, which he was forced to show so that the infuriated man could see that he had nothing to do with the hated or feared nationality or identity.

While thinking about all this, Adriana quickened her step. They were going by the giant aquarium—with sharks and rays, and all kinds of tropical fish swimming impassively, as if they were drugged—which went from the basement level to the third or fourth floor where they were walking, and perhaps just as long. Adriana turned the corner at the end of the aquarium, which led to the oriental souk area, through which you could get to the multiplex cinemas; he knew the way. Of late, he watched one or two movies per week there when he was tired of reading his novels and his work routine. Adriana stopped in front of a furniture and decor shop and, with her mobile, took quick pictures of some marquetry chairs and tables by the entrance, and quickly went on her way as if she were late for some work-related appointment. He also quickened his step; he could not waste time window shopping.

At the end of the oriental area, there was an annex dedicated to exclusive haute couture boutiques. Adriana walked on hurriedly, the echo of her steps bouncing against the walls. Suddenly, she stopped in front of a store, again to talk on her mobile. Tony kept a discreet distance and looked around. There were not many places to hide; all he could do was pretend to look at the shop windows that showed scandalously expensive items; the French atelier's dress he was looking at was priced at more than five thousand dollars. He doubted that Adriana was there shopping; she didn't seem to be interested in any of the shops. Perhaps she was just waiting for that call and needed to be in a place away from the noise of the rest of the mall. From her somewhat rigid and formal posture, Tony deduced that this time it was something important, though he couldn't hear more than an occasional yes or no in Spanish.

"So, it's true," she cried out suddenly. "I can't believe we belong to that horrible family of Jewish ancestry," she lamented after a pause. "The main thing is that this may prove that Grandfather Rafael didn't steal that bargueño but inherited it from his father, our great-grandfather, just as he said." Adriana suddenly turned around and scanned her surroundings, as if looking for something. Startled, Tony also turned around and started walking towards the exit. He felt a sort a panic; his heart raced fast. He heard Adriana walk behind him for a few steps but then she stopped. Perhaps she didn't recognize him. His shaven head and amber sunglasses might have fooled her…

TWENTY

On the way to Dubai from Abu Dhabi, Paola asked Esperanza if she remembered the stories that her grandfather told them when she visited during the end of the year holidays. Night was falling and highway traffic was dense; it was a Thursday, the last day of the week and the end of the month.

"I remember that he always told us the story of *The Last Sigh of the Moor*," said Esperanza, her gaze fixed on the road.

"Boabdil's," Paola whispered as if to herself.

"Did you forget it?"

"Completely. I swear, I would not have remembered myself."

"I find it odd," Esperanza remarked. "You knew several stanzas by heart. You always recited it to Grandpa, and he would give you a hug. I would get jealous because I saw that he loved you more than me."

"I don't understand how I could forget it."

"*Cry as a woman, unfortunate,*" Esperanza quoted.

"*The loss of the kingdom that you should have defended as a man,*" Paola added.

"*Cry, belittled,*" the two said in chorus.

"*And, with abrupt disdain badly compressed,*" Paola went on. "*Perhaps with deep desperate love, she turned away from the afflicted prince, and looking wrathful at Granada, she fled defeated, though not tamed.*"

"You still know it by heart!"

"Not all of it," Paola noted. "I don't remember what goes before or after. The lines came to me suddenly, as if they had been hiding in a dark corner of my mind."

"I'm sure you haven't forgotten the ending," Esperanza said, and had to suddenly change lanes; a white SUV with tinted windows swerved from the left lane into the one they were traveling, though at a slower speed. If Esperanza had not gone into the fast lane to the left, she might have hit the SUV from behind.

"*Wow,* that was scary," Paola cried out.

"It's someone who has been following us," Esperanza said and slowed down.

"Some idiot who doesn't like to see two women alone in a car."

"Perhaps, but I'll keep my distance."

"I don't see him anymore. Maybe he swerved that way because he had to get off the highway."

"I hope so," Paola said and put her palms together, like she was going to pray.

"*The whitest dove,*" Esperanza said after a moment.

"What are you talking about?"

"The stupid white SUV reminded me that there is a dove at the end of the story, which is not really a story but a poem…"

"*Soon, like the whitest dove,*" Paola recited. "*Far from the mountains, a rider could be seen over the last hill,*" she continued. "*It was the sad ghost of war; it was the perfidious power of Muhammad leaving the Spanish land…It was Boab-dil, wounded by the lightning that Pelayo struck in Asturias."*

"What good memory you have, cousin," Esperanza commented.

"It came to me suddenly."

"Bobadil the *bobito,* the little simpleton. Do you remember that I couldn't say Boabdil?"

"Yes, I remember now," Paola replied. "You would get the name backwards, and Grandpa would burst out laughing, and he would say, Boabdil was not a simpleton; that was *Simón el bobito*, the one in Rafael Pombo's poem."

"Yeah. When he used to tell us about Boabdil, we must have been eight or nine, right?"

"After that Christmas, Grandpa left, remember?"

"Yes, at that point begins Grandpa's mysterious life, which is what the historian is interested in," Esperanza said, stepping on the gas, and moved into one of the middle lanes; traffic was moving faster as they had left the city. "By the way, what did our dear Professor Rodrigues tell you? You talked to him for a while…"

"He told me to give it some thought, which is the same as nothing."

"But what did he tell you about the ornamental woodwork and the tortoise shell plate in the bargueño?"

"That it was very *interesting*, though it didn't surprise him, and then he told me that he and Professor Deenik, the old man with a beard who looks like grandfather, want to write an article about the bargueño and the *Fountain of the Lions.*"

"The one in the shopping mall?"

"That and the other one, the original, which is in the Alhambra Palace in Granada, Spain."

"And what does one thing have to do with the other?"

"I don't know, Esperanza. The two old men are nuts."

"He must have told you something."

"It's complicated because it turns out that the Fountain of the Lions at the mall is a copy, but *not* of the original when the Muslims were in power, but of the one that was in the palace centuries later when the Christians had already conquered Granada, and as part of the restoration work of the palace, had added to it another bowl on top, which totally changed its appearance. According to the professor, something similar happened to the bargueño; someone changed two pieces of ornamental woodwork, and the piece of wood on top, and completely transformed it. It's a big mess, cousin. And, I don't care."

Esperanza was about to say something, but in that instant, the white SUV that swerved in front of them before came to their left on the fast lane. Through its lowered right window, a brown-skinned young Arab wearing a *dishdasha* made a gesture to her with his hand, as if telling her to stop by the side of the road. Esperanza said, "*this one's crazy*," and stepped on the gas. The SUV's driver did the same, and in a matter of seconds, caught up with them. Esperanza stepped on the gas again with the same result. This time, she noticed that the back window was also lowered, and could see a slight, dark-skinned woman who looked more South Asian than Arab who wore a black abaya and sheila and had in her face a grimace of fear.

"Do you know that woman?" Paola asked, who from the first acceleration had her gaze fixed on the SUV.

"No, I've no idea who it could be. But this doesn't look good."

"You're going to kill us if you keep stepping on the gas," Paola said in a pleading tone.

"Don't worry cousin, I know what I'm doing."

On that section of the road there was a thin layer of mist hovering between the yellowish highway lights and the pavement. Paola began to feel a kind of vertigo before the open road ahead. The distance between the broken lines that marked the lanes was getting smaller; she thought that perhaps they would become solid at any moment. At some point, she looked at the speedometer that read one hundred and fifty kilometers per hour and rising; the round dial of Esperanza's leased Lexus went up to two hundred and ten. She wanted to say something but felt a lump in her throat. Meanwhile, Esperanza, with her foot on the gas, was concentrated. Her eyes going back and forth between the road ahead and the rearview mirror.

After a few minutes, the SUV got closer behind them, and the driver turned on the high beams, which blinded them for an instant. Esperanza changed lanes to the last one on her right, as if she were ready to take one of the exits, but there were none in that section.

"Slower," Paola begged.

"You're right, cousin. These assholes are not going to give up just like that. Call the police. Tell them someone is harassing us on the road, fifteen minutes out from Abu Dhabi heading to Dubai, and that we passed the last gas station five or so minutes ago."

Paola took the cell phone out of her bag but couldn't remember the police number at that moment. Esperanza looked at her sideways and said, "triple nine."

By then, the SUV was parallel to them, and again from the window, the young Arab made a sign with his hand, but now it was a fist—an ambiguous gesture—it could be a challenge or a celebration. A moment later, the driver accelerated ahead of them, swerved into their lane, and slowed down. Esperanza, who had anticipated the maneuver, put her foot on the brake, but it was not enough and had to veer further to the right, and all the way onto the road's shoulder, where she stopped the car. The driver of the SUV did the same and stopped a short distance from them. Esperanza put the car in reverse, drove back a few meters, and turned her high beams and hazard lights.

"Hang up the phone," she shouted.

"Startled by her cousin's tone," Paola did.

"Call Esteban. They can't be far away. When we left, they were saying their goodbyes."

Esteban answered at the first ring. Paola told him what was happening and repeated what she'd heard her cousin say about their location.

"Don't go anywhere," Esteban said after a short pause. I'm with Fernando; he knows what to do. We passed the last city exit, so we are close, ten minutes max. If someone leaves the SUV and tries to talk to you, tell Esperanza to back up slowly. Don't talk to them no matter what. Can you read their license plates?"

"No, Esteban. They are in Arabic, the numbers too."

"They must be Saudis. Don't talk to them no matter what," he repeated.

"Yeah, sure. Don't worry. Hurry up!"

The SUV's driver got out. He was a heavyset man, also in a *dishdasha*. He put a hand in front of his face to shield his eyes from the high beams and walked towards them.

Paola told Esperanza to back up. She said she would do it when she could see his face. The man stopped several meters from the car and shouted something in Arabic while making hand gestures, which Paola found threatening. He had a round face, bushy eyebrows, and just like the other man, he sported a goatee, though his was thin and ill groomed.

Esperanza backed up a few meters, which seemed to enrage the man who shouted again and made hand gestures.

Meanwhile, a police SUV, its flashing blue lights on, stopped behind them; they could see it on the car's video screen.

"I don't know if this is more trouble for us than for them," Esperanza said.

"Don't say that, cousin; we haven't done anything."

With the arrival of the police vehicle, the young man stopped making hand gestures and took a few steps back.

For a period of time that, to Paola, seemed to stretch forever, nobody did or said anything. From the patrol car came a beam of light. The heavyset man stood still, unperturbed. A little while after, Esteban's Mercedes pulled up to their side, then drove so as to park in front of the Lexus and stopped a few meters from the man. Then, several things happened at once. Fernando, who was driving Esteban's Mercedes got out, and in a loud voice, told the heavyset man in English to leave if he wanted to avoid getting into big trouble. At the same time, the policeman got out of his patrol car and walked towards them, following the beam of light. The policeman didn't stop by their Lexus, though, as Paola expected, but went straight over to the Mercedes' passenger side, and talked to Esteban, who had lowered his window. Meanwhile, the heavyset man turned around, in haste, and returned to his SUV and left. To Paola, the return of the man to his vehicle and his departure took place in slow motion. When she looked back at Esperanza, she was talking to Fernando.

"What a fright sweetie," she said.

He replied, "don't worry, everything is okay."

Esteban called Paola on her mobile. "Nothing happened, *Monita*. Tonight, you stay with me. Don't worry. There's no danger. Come drive with me. Fernando will take your cousin. Tomorrow we'll meet and have lunch in my apartment."

TWENTY-ONE

Paola could not sleep. In her mind, she saw again and again the face of the dark South Asian woman who was riding in the back of the white SUV that harassed them on the highway. She looked frightened, as if she feared for her life. Who was she to the two men riding up front? They didn't look as if they were related; the men were Arab, and she was not. She looked frail and gaunt, her eyes somewhat sunken but bright and expressive. Perhaps she was a maid; she had seen in her neighborhood women like her doing shopping at the supermarkets or taking children not their own to the nearby park. Paola closed her eyes but as she did, she felt her heart race. Suddenly, it occurred to her that the woman could be some sort of sex slave to the two men; Esperanza had told her stories like that. It was disgusting that men would go that far to satisfy their desires.

She got up and fumbled around. She did not want to wake Esteban, who was snoring intermittently. It was a soft snore whose rhythm increased or decreased at intervals, like an engine set up to go at two speeds. The bedroom door was open, and she tiptoed into the living room. She didn't have to turn on any of the lights; the glow of the city beyond was enough for her to see her way around the furniture. The apartment was on a high floor of a mixed-use building; offices were in the lower floors, apartments on the upper ones, and it was in the heart of Dubai's International Financial Center. It had a panoramic view of the city, which from that height looked like a small-scale mockup of itself. The road to Abu Dhabi, three or four blocks away, was like a piece of yellow ribbon dotted by tiny vehicles. Some had their flashing emergency blue lights on like the patrol car of the police officer who witnessed the threats of the heavyset man in *dishdasha*, only hours ago.

She walked around the living room, which was a large room with modern white leather furniture and a large Persian rug in faded blue tones, which Esteban told her had cost him a small fortune. Esteban loved luxury but didn't trust his taste; the decoration was the work of an Iranian interior designer who lived on the same floor on the other side of the building. He was a gay man who always wore white linen garments. He had dropped by after dinner to have a glass of wine, something he apparently did frequently. He lived alone and perhaps did not have many friends in the city. His visit had been somewhat strange, and after a brief conversation about nothing in particular—they did not talk about the incident on the highway—Esteban invited him to his study in one of the three rooms of the apartment, which he always kept locked under the pretext that they had some business to discuss, and after five minutes, they returned to the room where the Iranian said goodbye and promised he would drop by the following evening.

Paola was thinking about that moment while sitting on the sofa when Esteban turned on the lights.

"You can't sleep?" he asked.

"I can't get that woman's face out of my mind; like I told you, it made a deep impression on me."

"Do you want a whiskey?"

"No, thanks. I want to talk about what happened…"

"It'd be best if you forgot about it."

Paola felt suddenly angry. "How am I going to forget it? They almost killed us!"

"Sometimes things like this happen on the roads," Esteban said and pulled his right earlobe. "There are people who get offended by everything," he added with emphasis. "Perhaps Esperanza was driving aggressively; you always tell me that she drives like crazy."

"They were following us since we left Abu Dhabi."

"And what does that mean?"

"That it has to do with the Colombian soldiers."

"That's nonsense, Esteban said, while he poured himself a drink; the bar cart was next to the chair where he sat diagonally to her.

"Don't think I was born yesterday, Esteban. Those soldiers were in Yemen; perhaps the guys in the car were Yemeni; perhaps they wanted to tell us not to mess with their country."

"I don't know what you're talking about. That's nuts. Like I said, things like that happen on the roads sometimes; there are people who lose their temper at the slightest provocation."

"I thought Fernando knew them."

"No way. If he had known them, he would have spoken to them differently. Believe it or not, Fernando is a tough guy. He knows this country well and he has had to deal with all kinds of people."

"Fernando is military too…"

"He was in the Air Force. He retired before coming to this country. That's not a secret. You can ask Esperanza."

"Don't ever tell me again that what I say is nonsense. I don't know why you talk to me like that. What's clear is that you lie to me."

Esteban looked at her and frowned. "Okay. You're right," he said. "I'm going to tell you what I can tell you, which is not everything. You know that in business there are things that you can't talk about. We don't know who the guys in the SUV were, just like you, we suspect that what they did has to do with the presence of Colombian mercenaries in Yemen. That the car had Saudi plates doesn't surprise me; there are many Yemeni refugees in that country. What is happening in Yemen is very delicate, I mean politically very delicate. What's happening to the country is a real tragedy."

"But why get angry with us?"

"I don't know, *Monita*. It is a war situation…"

Paola didn't know what to say, and in spite of herself, she heaved a deep sigh. She felt that Esteban was telling her the truth, but she still felt annoyed with him. Esteban turned out to be the guy she thought he was; a man of the world, educated and successful with virtues that made him attractive. He was the type of man she always thought ideal for her, or perhaps the type of man who was ideal for her as she was before; the entrepreneurial Adriana of her last year in Japan, the Adriana who was not afraid of anything, the lioness that her grandfather would have wanted her to be. But she wasn't like that anymore, she told herself. Or was she? What was happening to her? Did she doubt herself now? What the hell was wrong with her?

"Why don't we change the subject and talk about the barg ueño," Esteban proposed. "I heard that you rejected the offer of the law firm in Bogotá that I recommended."

"I'm represented by a law firm in the United States."

"They'll charge you an arm and a leg."

"It's pro bono; they get a cut if we win, that was the deal. We'll see."

"What else? I have the impression that you don't tell me everything."

"It's complicated," Paola said. "To make the story short, they made it clear that the museum has no compelling arguments to keep the bargueño, which means that they'll return it to us. We had to provide them with the results of DNA testing, and everything went well. Once we finish with the paperwork, I'll put it up for sale. There are two parties interested in buying it, one in Spain and the other here."

"A local buyer? An Emirati?"

"He's an Egyptian, a professor at a university in Dubai."

"Sheikh Fardan's puppet, the little man who goes crazy with the Russian models from your agency," Esteban said in a mocking tone. "But, seriously, if I were you, I wouldn't sell it just like that," he added.

"Oh, really," Paola said with sarcasm. "What would you do?"

"If it's such an important piece of furniture that Sheikh Fardan wants to buy it, I would put it up for sale at an auction in New York or London. I could help you with that. I know people in Europe who move in those circles."

Paola looked at Esteban, and again felt angry as she'd felt minutes before, though even more so, in such a way that made her tense up her arms and hands. She wanted to shout at him not to meddle with her affairs.

"I'd rather you don't help me," she said and felt a sudden tremor on her lips.

"As you wish, *Monita*," Esteban said and came to her side on the couch. Paola noticed the smell of whiskey, which seemed to emanate from his body and not from the glass in his hand.

"I think it's better that we don't see each other for a while," Paola said, almost without thinking as if by instinct. Esteban moving from his armchair to her side made something within her, hidden until now, explode.

"Do you think that by being with me someone will hurt you?"

"No, Esteban. What I want to say is that there is something between us that doesn't work, and we need time to think about whether we should be together or not."

Esteban said nothing

"You kill me with those words," Esteban said and drank what was left of his drink.

"No. It's me who's dying."

"I see that you are upset."

Just then, far in the horizon, appeared three combat helicopters, one after the other, the roar of their turbines just a dry murmur. The sky was clearing in the distance; it would dawn soon.

Esteban made with his hand the figure of a gun, which he shot with his thumb, pointing at the aircraft.

"I'm going to sleep for a while longer," he said and yawned. "In a few hours, Fernando and I will figure out what happened on the road. It won't happen again. I can promise you that."

Esteban made as if he was about to give her a kiss, something she no longer cared for, but instead got up and waved goodbye to her.

"I'll stay here a while longer," she said. "And you can go to hell," she added under her breath as he turned around.

TWENTY-TWO

Tony searched the Internet with the words bargueño and Jewish. He was intrigued by what he heard Adriana say at the mall a few days ago about a Jewish ancestor who would apparently make her part of a family that she called horrible, though it would somehow also go to prove that her grandfather had not stolen the bargueño. It was odd because only a few weeks ago, he did a similar search with the words bargueño and Al-Andalus after the dinner at the Moroccan restaurant where Professor Al Morsi claimed that the bargueño that Fardan wanted to buy was an example of Islamic art that flourished in Al-Andalus. A few weeks before that, he searched for bargueño and Colombia hours after he was done with the translation of the Colombian documents he had made for the Fardans.

In each search he had found links to academic and journalistic texts, and to photographs of bargueños representative of various styles, but it was not yet clear to him what the origin of that piece of furniture was. An article in a Spanish academic journal claimed that it was quintessentially

Spanish Golden Age, that is, from the sixteenth to the seventeenth centuries, although it admitted a Moorish influence; the Museo del Virreinato in Bogotá's website suggested a Syrian and Andalusian origin, as Professor Al Morsi had said, but claimed that the correct term to designate the type of furniture they had on display in the museum was *escritorio*, 'writing table'; and an English auction house's magazine speculated that the marquetry technique of the Spanish and New World bargueños originated in the Roman Empire, and had remarkable aesthetic development in various parts of Europe, especially in Renaissance Italy. In short, the bargueño could be from everywhere, or from nowhere in particular.

While meditating on these past findings, he realized that within the results of his new search there was one that led to a novel written by a nineteenth-century Spanish philologist about an Andalusian bargueño that contained the true key to the secrets of the Kabbalah and Hasidic Judaism. He clicked on the link which took him to Project Gutenberg's webpage, an open access virtual library. He scanned the first two pages and decided to download it to his computer. He had not read a novel in Spanish for a long time; it would help him improve his vocabulary. He would start reading it that same evening, and he could finish it over the long weekend. Monday was a religious holiday, and the government announcement was explicit that restaurants and bars would be closed, with a few exceptions.

While his computer was downloading the file, he looked closely at the images on the cover of the book. On the back was the Kabbalistic symbol of the tree of life, and on the front, a drawing of an older man with a beard who sported a kind of turban. The drawing, or the character it represented, seemed familiar; perhaps he had seen it before, though he could not be sure where. He always had a taste for antique books on esoteric topics, such as this, published in Mexico City in nineteen-twelve. Perhaps it was one of the books he was browsing at an antiquarian bookstore in Barcelona last year when he was on vacation. Or perhaps he saw it at someone's house, though not in Dubai. He was sure of that as the vague memory was farther away; it had to have been in Tokyo. He looked again at the drawing of the bearded man on the cover, which was actually an engraving, and suddenly remembered that he saw it in a photograph in Adriana's apartment. It was on the cover of a book that her grandfather, a man who had a full head of white hair and a beard, carried in his hand while he hugged her. Perhaps it was a gift; she must have been thirteen or fourteen. His memory of the day he saw the picture got sharper; he remembered jokingly asking her whether the book her grandfather had in his hand was his biography or his autobiography, given the similarity between her grandfather and the man on the cover, and Adriana replied that she wished it had been so because she missed him so much.

He felt nostalgic for that day with Adriana. That night, after making love, they talked about many things. Their business partnership was just beginning, as well as their relationship as a couple. At some point, she told him anecdotes about her grandfather who apparently had a nomadic life, full of adventures, for whom she felt a deep affection and admiration. It was something new for him to hear someone talk like that about a relative. He had never felt anything like that for anyone in his family, indeed for anyone at all.

With his gaze fixed on the virtual cover of the book his computer was still downloading, he wondered what kind of man Adriana's grandfather had been. All of the anecdotes she told him indicated he was a man of many talents, though somewhat eccentric and mysterious. If the book he was holding in the photo was, in effect, about Kabbalistic secrets, the question arose as to whether her grandfather was an initiate in these subjects, or if he only knew them superficially. Apart from helping to dispel any doubts that would remain about why her grandfather had that bargueño, the answer to that question could influence the assessment of the piece, which perhaps, like that of the novel, could be linked to mystic Judaism, and also in its appraisal, although it was not clear if it was for better or worse. In any case, Adriana's inheritance was extraordinary. Not only for the historical value of the bargueño, but for the complicated baggage with which it came; the Jewish part of herself that made her part of that family she called horrible, which made her history extend backwards in time, and was something that could give more substance and texture to her life.

In contrast, his family seemed to have no past at all. He never met his grandparents as they had all died before he was born. There were no memories of them, not even photographs. His parents rarely mentioned them; it was as if they had not figured in their lives—or just superficially—or as if their deaths had erased them completely. He tried to imagine what his paternal grandfather looked like. His father had once told him that he was an army officer during the earlier years of *La Violencia*, the period of political violence in a faraway Andean province, and that from him they had both inherited his gray eyes and hooked nose. He closed the search engine and opened his virtual photo album where he had a few pictures of his family. There were ten or twelve photographs he rarely looked at. Until today he had no particular reason for doing so. In a photograph of his First Communion party where he was with his father, he focused on the eyes and nose, and just as on past occasions, he did not see a resemblance, though it occurred to him that the resemblance would become evident now that he turned thirty-five, the age his father would have been when they took that picture.

He was about to take his computer to the bathroom mirror to compare his father's face to his own, when he saw an SMS text from Wendy in which she said that the committee meeting was once again running late because of Al Morsi. Poor Wendy, he thought. She had been busy all week editing her proposal for a summer course exchange program at two universities in Philadelphia because Al Morsi—whom the administration had appointed at the last minute to the committee—did not like the courses in political science and literature that Wendy had chosen. Apparently, Al Morsi had claimed that the courses were not appropriate for young Muslim women, although he did not say why; it was clearly his personal judgement.

Once he compared the picture of his father to his own image in the mirror, he realized that despite his shaved head, he was beginning to resemble his father, not only in the face but also in his bearing in the somewhat rigid, almost military, way of standing, something that Wendy had jokingly made him aware of the other day. Even so, it was a misleading resemblance. He could have inherited many things from his father, but he could not conceive of a person so different from him in everything else, in his way of thinking, in his attitude towards life, and in his way of relating to people.

Back at the dining room table with his computer, he was surprised to see red and orange tinted clouds on the horizon. It was almost seven o'clock on his computer's digital clock. He had forgotten to call his friend Pablo to finish the interview about life in Dubai! He opened his email and sent him an apology message with a promise that he would call him the next day without fail.

He went out to the balcony and sat on the small wicker sofa to watch the sunset, something he did with Wendy whenever he stayed over. From the creek came gusts of a warm breeze and a sharp saline smell. He felt a little restless and disturbed, both because he forgot to call his friend in Tokyo, and because of Wendy's unusual delay. That night they had agreed to have dinner at a new Japanese restaurant in the nearby shopping mall to celebrate the end of the work week. Although now that he thought about it, it was not such a good idea because, as a holiday, the restaurants would be full of people, and they would have to wait a long time to get a good table.

Something on the street made him look down, and he noticed that there was a line of vehicles, mostly SUVs and some taxis, waiting for their turns to unload passengers and luggage at the luxury hotel residences next door. Probably families from the Gulf states or from Saudi Arabia that came to Dubai to spend religious holidays.

Scanning the horizon, he saw the Burj Khalifa begin its evening light show. Tonight, it consisted of multicolored Arabic letters that wriggled from the bottom upwards around the tower as if it were some sort of advertising. Although, it could well be a prayer celebrating the religious holiday.

TWENTY-THREE

Two soft knocks outside the office door startled Tony. It occurred to him that it was the police who came to confiscate the accounting ledgers whose pages he was taking pictures of so that he could, at leisure—in the privacy of his apartment or wherever he happened to be—continue to try to figure out the money laundering secrets the ledgers were hiding within. He thought about asking who it was, but he changed his mind, crammed the books the best way he could into his desk drawer, and said, "come in."

"Sorry to interrupt," Professor Deenik said, who today was accompanied by a balding, Levantine-looking man sporting a salt and pepper goatee. "This is my esteemed colleague, Professor Tomás Rodrigues."

Tony got up and shook hands with Deenik's colleague whose face seemed familiar. He was sure he had seen him before, though he couldn't remember where or when.

Deenik apologized for dropping by unexpectedly and asked him whether he could spare them ten minutes for a chat. "We'd like to ask you a few questions, if you don't mind," he added.

Tony replied he would be happy to and ordered a pot of tea and some pastries.

"I want to get straight to the point," Deenik said. "Do you work for Fardan Al Fardan?"

"No, not anymore," Tony stated and felt somewhat uncomfortable; it was something that happened recently, an episode he wanted to forget. "I did some translations for them a while ago, but nothing more," he added. "Why do you ask?"

"Because of a series of events related to each other. Forgive me if I sound cryptic. You'll see soon what I mean, I promise. Let's start with Wendy. Do you know what happened?"

"No one knows for sure," Tony said. "Everything at work was going smoothly—with ups and downs, of course—until yesterday afternoon when she called to tell me she'd been fired and had fifteen days to leave the country for good. She's being deported."

"Did she say why?" Rodrigues asked.

"The person who fired her, the head of Human Resources doesn't know. He said that word of it came *all the way from the top*, not of the university, but of the government."

"It was as I'd feared," Deenik said and rubbed his beard. "It's not the first time that something like this has happened," he added pensively. "As I told you once, people come and go in this country. From the cases I've heard about at the university, it's always the same thing; the order came from the top."

"I'm leaving too," said Tony.

"I'm also sorry to hear that," Deenik said and arched his eyebrows. "May I ask why?"

"This morning I received an email from the Ministry of Labor informing me that I won't be able to renew my work visa, which expires next month, and that the decision is final, without recourse for appeal."

"How odd. It may be a coincidence," Deenik said and scratched his temple.

"It could be," Rodrigues said with an ironic smirk. "But since we don't know *what* or *who* is at the top pulling the strings, I guess we'll never know."

Tony looked at Rodrigues and felt again that he knew him from somewhere; his face was a bit like his without any particular features that gave a clear clue to his origin. His accent was vaguely like Wendy's; perhaps he was an Australian of Spanish origin, maybe from the Canary Islands. He had a Canarian friend in Tokyo who looked like him.

"Be that as it may, there is a character that seems to be behind this and other woes," Deenik said, addressing Tony. "Do you remember that I told you something about an Egyptian professor who wrote an article about Muslim bestiaries?"

"Yes, I remember," Tony replied. "Wendy also told me about him because they work together in some academic committee." Tony was going to say that he'd met him in person, but he changed his mind; he thought it was not wise at the time.

"Oh, of course," Deenik said and frowned. "They put him on all the important committees. But that's not all. A couple of days ago he was appointed dean of the college, an appointment that was made in secret; it didn't follow the university's policies and procedures and is in violation of the terms of international accreditation. In any case, this character, the distinguished professor Al Morsi, who is an intolerant man, not to mention his other *qualities* not relevant to my point today, has a mandate to purge the college of everything that is not aligned with the ideology and desires—not of the senior administration who in fact are just puppets—but of the person that this Egyptian mistakenly calls *Dr.* Fardan Al Fardan…"

Tony couldn't help but laugh. "I beg your pardon, professor," he said. "It's not my intention to make light of this, which is really tragic, but Wendy already knew that."

"That it was Fardan who pulled the strings?"

"She's known Fardan for a long time, and she gets along with him and his son."

"Oh, I didn't know," Deenik said and looked at Professor Rodrigues who nodded; maybe it was something he suspected. "How little we professors know of what goes on at the university," Deenik added in a tone of amazement.

"But, if Wendy gets along with Fardan, father and son, why did they fire her?" Rodrigues asked and took a sip of his cup of tea.

"Wendy told me that days ago, when classes started after the long weekend, a rumor began to run in the university that she was a sexual pervert, and that she had seduced both male and female students", Tony said in a tone loaded with irony.

"I wouldn't be surprised if Al Morsi is behind that rumor," Deenik said. "They didn't get along. Wendy told me that last semester, when Al Morsi was hired, he went to her office—which is in the library but has nothing to do with it, you only have to look at the name plate on the door—and without even saying hello, started complaining that his books were not in the library's collection. Wendy asked him not to yell at her, and Al Morsi became enraged and asked if she knew who he was and told her that he would file a complaint to the Provost. Fortunately, a student who was around explained to Al Morsi—in Arabic—that Wendy was not part of the library staff, and he reluctantly let the matter go. Wendy complained to the head of Human Resources, and Al Morsi had to apologize, something he seems not to like at all."

"Wow. Wendy told me about the incident, but not about the bit with the head of Human Resources," Tony said. "Good for her! In any case, going back to the rumor, it seems that some of the students took it all the way to the Prime Minister's office."

"That explains everything!" Deenik said and put a hand to his face.

"It's a shame," Rodrigues said. "The few times I had to work with her, I found her very competent."

"Wendy told me that you have also had problems with Al Morsi," Tony said.

"Yes, indeed," said Deenik. "It was just what I was going to tell you. In a faculty meeting about using government funds for academic research, Al Morsi hinted that my dear colleague and I were writing an article that compromised the integrity of some religious precepts, though he didn't explain what precepts or give any evidence to prove it. He did have the decency not to mention our names. In any case, his colleagues in the department of Islamic studies began to murmur out loud that that could not be tolerated given the delicate current political situation. Here, everything must be considered in relation to the *delicate* political situation, which is also a matter of religion. But that does not matter; Professor Rodrigues and I are going to resign. I'm already of retirement age, and Professor Rodrigues has a visiting appointment and can return to his job without any problems. All this arose around a hypothesis I had the poor judgement to share with one of Al Morsi's Egyptian colleagues about the Jewish origin of the Fountain of the Lions in the famous palace of the Alhambra in Granada, Spain."

"I see," Tony said. "But your research is also about a Colombian colonial piece of furniture, isn't it?"

"Ah! Now I understand where you fit into all this," Rodrigues interjected. "The translations you made were about that piece of furniture, right?"

"That's right. I didn't know that you were investigating its origin."

"That, by the way, is still a mystery," Deenik noted.

"I thought you had solved that…"

"We are not experts in that area," Deenik explained. "Our research is not about establishing the origin of anything; that requires another type of work for which we are not qualified. Our article, which we have not yet finished, is a reflection on the protocols for curatorship in museums whose mission is to preserve the historical heritage of their regions or countries. Perhaps our critical tone is an affront to people like Al Morsi, who are more inquisitors than researchers and are only interested in defending some orthodoxy, be it religious or academic."

"If you don't mind going back to what you did for Mr. Fardan," Rodrigues said. "What kind of documents did you have to translate?"

Tony replied that it was a will with a list of bequests and other related documents.

"The list included some bargueños?"

"Yes, and two bestiaries."

A smile appeared on Rodrigues' face.

"Did the list say what kind of bestiaries they were?" Deenik asked.

"It just said they were medieval bestiaries."

"There we could find the answers to all our questions," Rodrigues said.

"I don't understand what one thing has to do with the other," Tony said.

"We recently realized that the engravings of one of the bargueños were copied not from one but from several bestiaries," Deenik said.

"If we could examine the bestiaries, we could have a better idea of who made that particular bargueño," Rodrigues added.

"We will have to ask Paola if she also inherited the bestiaries," Deenik said.

"Which Paola?" Tony asked and crossed his arms.

"Paola is the young Colombian who inherited the bargueños."

"Paola is Adriana Paola," Tony said.

"Do you know her?" Rodrigues asked.

"I know who she is. That's all."

For a few moments they sat in silence.

"Dear Tony," Deenik said. "Allow me the honor of throwing a small party for you and Wendy in my apartment tomorrow. If you don't have any other commitments, of course…"

TWENTY-FOUR

Tony gazed towards Bank Street crossing a few blocks away from the tourist information booth at a creek side shopping area near the foreign consulates. It was a hot May morning, and the sky was overcast with a thin blanket of opaque gray clouds. In the parking area in front of the entrance sat a double decker bus of a tour company from which a group of mostly European tourists were getting off, many of them wearing sun hats and dark glasses. It was the first time Tony was there, even though it was relatively close to his apartment, fifteen minutes away by foot. It was a new tourist and shopping area built in old Dubai style with adobe walls, large wooden doors, and wind towers that housed high-end boutiques and a few restaurants and coffee shops, which gave it an air of an oriental bazaar theme park.

He had been waiting for nearly a half hour for Adriana, who at first did not want to see him, though changed her mind at the last minute. Perhaps Esperanza, who had served as an intermediary, had talked her into it. Wendy, who was in better spirits after the debacle at the university, thought it a good idea. She told him that bringing closure to the partnership and relationship he had forged with Adriana in Tokyo would do well to the relationship that they were building together, which would be put to a test in the coming months when they no longer had the economic stability that their jobs in Dubai gave them.

He was still thinking about it when he saw Adriana walk directly towards him, an expression of doubt and amazement on her face.

"You look like someone else!" she cried out. "If you had not said you'd be waiting for me right here, I would not have recognized you. The bald head fits you very well. You should have done it before," she added and gave him a friendly smile, which somehow, he thought unusual in her.

"You also look different, and the new look suits you," Tony said and hugged her. "I'm very happy to see you," he added.

"Same here," Adriana said and took a step back, perhaps aware of the social etiquette in Dubai, or because she wanted to make it clear that she did not want any kind of intimacy with him.

They went to one of the cafés at the end of the shopping area near the Metro. They ordered two cappuccinos and got a table overlooking the street.

"I heard that you solved your problems with the bosses," Tony said and looked Adriana in the eye. He thought she was wearing colored contact lenses, though remembered right away that her honey-colored eyes were like that, their tint varied a little depending on the kind of light. Adriana told him that the day they met; it was odd he had forgotten about it.

"I guess Vladimir told you," Adriana replied and frowned slightly, perhaps annoyed with his gaze. "Was he the one who told you that I was in Dubai? My cousin Esperanza didn't tell me how you found me."

"It wasn't Vladimir, Adriana. It's a long story…"

"But I have no time for that," Adriana said and shook her head.

"You're right," he said. "I guess you have a busy day…"

Adriana nodded and smiled again. It was a feigned smile, not the spontaneous, friendly, ear-to-ear smile of a few moments ago.

"I learned it from Wendy," Tony said, and for some reason he had to cough; his throat was dry.

"Wendy, my cousin Esperanza's friend?"

"Yes, she's my girlfriend," he added and took a sip of his cappuccino.

"Oh! I understand now," Adriana said in a tone loaded with sarcasm, and crossed her arms.

"It's something that happened…"

"You don't have to explain anything to me," Adriana interrupted. "We were not engaged or anything like that. Neither were we *girlfriend* and *boyfriend,*" she said a little louder, her tone full of sarcasm.

Tony told himself it was time to apologize to Adriana, but he didn't know what to say.

"I hope you don't treat her like you treated me," Adriana said, a trace of anger on her face. "Did you know her in Tokyo? Esperanza told me that she lived there for several years."

Tony shook his head.

"Are you thinking of partnering up with her in Dubai?"

"I won't deny that I thought about it. It seemed like a good idea, but things have changed."

Adriana looked at him with a grimace of doubt. "I guess you'll have your reasons, but from a practical standpoint, things are easier in this country. There are no taxes, nobody complains, and as far as I know, there is no mafia you have to pay a weekly fee to for protection. Besides, ours is a modeling agency, not a shady exotic dancer agency."

"And do you think there is a lot of difference?"

"Of course there is a lot of difference," Adriana replied. "As a man, you wouldn't understand. Your world is right next to mine, but it may as well be in another galaxy. I do what I can to survive and to get ahead. I can't afford to reject the opportunities that are given to me; you know well my circumstances. Besides, everything is perfectly legal; the models have their visas in order, Esperanza's contacts take care of all that."

"Not everything that glitters is gold, Adriana."

"There is no perfect place in the world, Tony."

"You're right. By the way, why did you choose this place to meet?"

"Because the beauty salon that I like is close to here. I hardly ever come to this side of the city."

"Did you know that right now we are practically in the heart of the red-light district?"

"In this neighborhood?"

"It doesn't look it, right?"

"How do you know?"

"Vladimir told me not to come here at night."

"And, you didn't listen to him."

"At first yes, of course. Vladimir knows Dubai well. Remember that he was here for several months making investments for the big boss."

"And after that?"

"Oh, after a while, I started to explore a bit on my own.

Do you see the intersection over there, where the metro station is? Vladimir calls it the *Bermuda Triangle*."

"That's what he used to call the area with the strip joints and love hotels in Kabukichō in Tokyo…"

"Same thing here, Adriana. Whoever falls into their dens never makes it back home."

"That *does* surprise me," Adriana said, and again, looked out the window towards the Metro station. She bit her lower lip, something she did after hearing bad news or when contemplating an undesirable scenario.

"I thought that was illegal in Dubai."

"It probably is. But, as the saying goes, we all have skeletons in the closet."

"Esperanza told me that there were such things, but all very camouflaged, never in plain sight."

"Well, it is."

For a moment, Tony and Adriana were silent.

"Was it you who was interviewed for that half-page article in the newspaper?" Adriana asked suddenly and raised her eyebrows.

"What newspaper are you talking about?"

"One of Bogota's, dummy. Where else?"

"I didn't know that it came out in Colombia."

"Oh, so it was *you*. I guess it must have been your Peruvian pal in Tokyo, the one who works for the Spanish news agency, right? You gave him a report, warts and all, of Dubai's underworld, which you know so well…"

"It could have been anyone who knows Dubai well…"

"You're really full of surprises," Adrianna blurted. "Why did you do it? Someone told me that caused a stir in the Colombian Embassy in Abu Dhabi, also in the Spanish one. You created a small diplomatic crisis, according to Esperanza."

"Did you read it?"

"Yes. Nobody in this country is going to like it."

"There is nothing in the article that is not true."

"How did you know about the Colombian soldiers?"

"Don't tell me you did not know."

"Of course I knew, don't think I keep my head in the sand," Adriana retorted and took several sips of the cappuccino; she had not touched it so far. "Be that as it may, there are many people who are not going to like that article."

"Only those who can read it in Spanish."

Adriana looked at him and made a face of distrust.

"I have the feeling there's something else you haven't told me, Tony."

"You're right, there's something else. I found out by chance that your inheritance was an antique piece of furniture from the colonial era."

"Oh yeah? Who told you?"

"A little bird."

"Don't fuck with me, Tony. Tell me!"

Tony recounted to her how he had met Fardan Jr. through Wendy; about the translations he did for his father where there was a mention of an inheritance that included some bargueños, and how Fardan and Al Morsi wanted the bargueño to be put up for sale in a public auction that they could manipulate to their liking.

Adriana, who looked at him impassively, suddenly arched her eyebrows. Perhaps she didn't know anything about Fardan's intentions or that Al Morsi was involved.

"And how did you know it was my inheritance?"

"Tying loose ends here and there. You know how I like detective novels."

Adriana looked at him out of the corner of her eye. "I don't believe you, Tony."

"I've never lied to you, Adriana."

"In any case, the matter is already settled. I sold it to a relative."

"To the historian?"

"I see you're well informed," she said and squinted her eyes.

"Why don't we talk as friends?"

"Now you want us to be friends?"

"Forgive me, Adriana. I know I screwed up. I should have pleaded your case with the bosses, but I didn't know how—I couldn't come up with anything—perhaps deep inside I also wanted to get away. I didn't have any way to get in touch with you. You left everything behind, even your phones."

"They could have easily traced me with the mobiles."

"You could have sent me an email."

"I closed my accounts and deleted all my contacts."

"And you decided to forget about your friends."

"Not my *girlfriends*. They were the ones who told me that you had not done anything for me, that you had left, that Vladimir had helped you. They also heard that you went to Bangkok."

"They were right about everything, though Bangkok was just a stopover. I barely spent a day in the city."

"So, we've been in Dubai about the same time."

"And we each went our separate ways. Your inheritance changed everything."

Adriana crossed her arms and sighed. "What do you want, Tony? I don't understand your sudden interest."

"I'm leaving Dubai for good in a couple of days, and I wanted to see you one last time.

"Don't be so dramatic, Tony. Why are you going to leave if you have the easiest job in the world, not to mention the perfect partner?"

Tony told her what had happened to Wendy at the

university, and of his surprise when he learned that his work contract would not be renewed.

"Do you think it's because of the article?"

"There is no way of knowing. It could be. It's also possible that they're watching us at this moment, perhaps also recording our conversation."

Adriana waved her right hand in front of her face in the Japanese way of saying no, which in this case meant that what she had just heard was nonsense.

Tony crossed his arms and looked Adriana in the eye.

"You really don't know?"

Tony shook his head.

"So, what are you going to do?" Adriana asked and ran her fingers over her earlobe. She was wearing jade earrings she had bought at a flea market in Tokyo. He had gone with her that day to help out as an interpreter; they had just met, and Adriana still didn't communicate well in English or Japanese. "Wendy got a job at a university in Okinawa, but the semester doesn't start until October, so we'll have to hang out in Thailand and Malaysia until then. As for me, I could teach English and Spanish; that's what I did before my stint in Roppongi."

"Doesn't Wendy have a family in Australia?"

"Her parents passed a few years ago; she only has a few uncles and cousins, but just as with me, she prefers to keep her distance."

"I'm going to Colombia for the summer. The agency doesn't have much work then. I'm also dying to see my parents."

"Will you stay in your town?"

"Yes, but I will also travel with the relative I mentioned, the historian. We are second cousins; we have the same great-grandfather. Sara, my cousin, wants to research the history of our shared family, especially my grandfather's life who is her great uncle. She wants to write a book about him. She says that we'll understand the true value of the bargueño I inherited when we understand the history of its making."

"The history of its making," Tony repeated. "Your cousin sounds like an interesting person to be around."

"I think so too."

"I wish you luck, Adriana."

"And I to you."

Acknowledgments

Special thanks to Colleen Quigley, Maria Mercedes Gómez, Federico Vélez and Robert Garot.